My Story

Confessions of a Swinger

Nicci Greene

authorHOUSE

AuthorHouse™ UK Ltd.
500 Avebury Boulevard
Central Milton Keynes, MK9 2BE
www.authorhouse.co.uk
Phone: 08001974150

© 2009 Nicci Greene. All rights reserved.

No part of this book may be reproduced, stored in a retrieval system, or transmitted by any means without the written permission of the author.

First published by AuthorHouse 11/4/2009

ISBN: 978-1-4490-3842-7 (sc)

This book is printed on acid-free paper.

Contents

Chapter One – How We Met	1
Chapter Two – Our First Time	16
Chapter Three – Getting Together Was Complicated	32
Chapter Four – Married Life	36
Chapter Five – Porn	40
Chapter Six – Threesome	47
Chapter Seven – Swinging	54
Chapter Eight – Keys In A Bowl	61
Chapter Nine – It Didn't Always Work Out	71
Chapter Ten - The Young Guy	77
Chapter Eleven- Two Guys, One Night	82
Chapter Twelve - The Elderly Man	97
Chapter Thirteen – My Husband's Boss	105
Chapter Fourteen – The Photographer	120
Chapter Fifteen – The Internet	139
Chapter Sixteen - The Villa	148
About the Author	177

Chapter One — How We Met

I met my husband at work, he was my boss and when I first met him he made me shudder not with excitement but with fear. When he entered the room he had such a presence that everyone scurried around pretending to work hard at least when he was there. I didn't look at him in a sexual way and don't even know if I was attracted to him at first. When I think back now though he did look awfully dashing in his suit. He was a tall man with short dark hair, a slim build with broad shoulders and carried a suit very well. He always wore dark suits but with bright ties that looked like he had a fun side but that never showed in work. He was always serious, professional and demanding but I guess he allowed his guard to drop sometimes near me which at first I didn't notice. It was a while before I realised that he spent more time in our office than the others and even longer before I realised he spent more time around my desk than anywhere else.

His presence did not allow idle chit chat nor did his demeanour make it possible to make small talk with him so it was a surprise when he said good morning to me or asked how my day had been. It was only after he spoke to me that I saw something in him, a softer side or possibly even a sexy side as the corners of his mouth curled when he spoke to me, almost cracking a smile.

He was young to be in such a respected position but I didn't realise he was only a few years my senior at first. He was so professional and good at his job that he seemed like he was in his thirties rather than his twenties.

I began to wonder about him. Did he have any friends or life even, outside of work? He was always first in and last out and if deadlines had to be achieved he was there all evening with the staff on overtime.

He never asked me to do the overtime as it was always the more experienced older staff that he could trust to work quickly and accurately probably so that he didn't have to be there all night.

Sometimes I felt left out. It wasn't that I needed the money but it would've been nice and I began to look forward to his half hearted smiles and pleasantries.

At the time I lived with my boyfriend who was his opposite, scruffy and hard compared to the well groomed presence of my boss. My boyfriend was from my home town and had urged me to go for the job in the city. Something he probably regrets to this day. He worked in a factory in our home town and although he was out early each morning he was home well before me in the evenings. Despite that I was expected to cook the dinner after walking half a mile from the train station to get home.

I didn't mind then because of the way I was brought up.

Where I lived and came from this was normal. Most of the women from the older generation hadn't gone out to work, however, nowadays it was expected that the woman would not only go out to work but also do all of the housework and cooking. Being honest I never thought anything of it at the time.

We lived in a flat above a butchers shop and occasionally in the summer the smell of rotting meat from the bins put me off eating. It was understandable then that I enjoyed my work and I looked forward to seeing my boss and meeting different people from those in my home town. The women I met were very different from those I had grown up with or been used to mixing with and were all very independent. Some even lived together in their own apartment in the city. They didn't have go home to cook and instead went out for meals together and ordered take-aways. It seemed such a glamorous life compared to mine and I wondered about my boss. I wondered where he lived.

The mystery of my boss heightened his appeal to me, as did our little interactions but it wasn't until my annual review that he really took hold of me.

I walked into his office and sat in the chair in front of his desk that was placed there for each person being reviewed. I was nervous, not because of him but because of the situation, my first review. He often made me nervous too but on this occasion his smile as I entered made him seem less scary. He briefly chatted about my progress and remarked on how his seniors had been impressed with his reports of me. He told me that I had a great future and my head grew with his compliments even though my face grew warmer as he stared into my eyes when he spoke.

It was only then that I noticed his intense but beautiful blue eyes and his exceptionally long eyelashes. I knew I should have been concentrating on his chat but my concentration waned further as my gaze drifted to his mouth. As I watched the words coming out I noticed his lips which I thought were perfectly formed and looked both soft and moist. I found myself imagining kissing him until I pulled myself together as he barked his question, 'What do you think?'

It took me by surprise as I wasn't paying attention to what he'd said prior to that. My face was feeling hotter as I became more and more embarrassed. I knew it was red because I could almost see the glow rising to my eye level and I could feel the heat burning my cheeks. He didn't answer which made it worse. Then he stood up and walked around his desk towards me. My legs were crossed but they tightened blocking off the circulation and trapping the blood in my face making me look even more embarrassed. He sat on the desk in front of me. He was so close my leg almost touched his. I think I actually wanted our legs to touch and I wanted the tension to release out of my legs but they remained stiff.

Then he spoke again, 'We have some overtime coming up if you are interested?' 'I could help train you on the other system which would help with your promotion'. 'Promotion!?' I exclaimed, making it obvious that I hadn't been paying attention. 'Yes' he replied, 'Like I said we think you would make a good office manager and the extra training will help you pass the tests.'

I was pleased and the tension disappeared as he was being kind, not authoritarian or scary but helpful and kind. His gesture to come from behind his desk was not to make me feel more uncomfortable but to put me at ease. He talked on about the new position, what it entailed and the salary increase but I focused only on the extra money. I imagined a new life in the city, in my own apartment but when I imagined it my boyfriend wasn't there with me.

'So do you think you can handle the challenge?', he asked and as he did so he put out his hand. I stood to face him and although he was still sitting on the desk we were both at eye level because he was so tall. 'Yes', I said, 'I would love it'. 'I knew you would', he said with confidence and as his hand stretched out I put mine in his to shake it. 'Welcome to the world of management' he said just as our hands met. His felt warm, soft and gentle not like my boyfriend's and the hand shake wasn't firm it was loose and almost sensual. It seemed to last a long time and as our hands parted they stroked each other gently.

At that precise moment I realised that I fancied my boss!

I wanted him to hold my hand forever. I looked into his beautiful eyes and then at his beautiful lips and I very nearly leant in to kiss him but I managed to turn and leave the room with some dignity intact.

I worked the overtime, as suggested, much to the dislike of my boyfriend who moaned about his dinner so much that I actually prepared food the night before so it would be there for him the next day, if I wasn't coming home. After all I didn't want his mother giving off to me when I saw her for not looking after my man. That's what it was like in my town. My own mother would've probably given off to me too had she thought he would be left, without dinner after a day at the factory.

It was mostly on a Thursday night but sometimes also a Wednesday and true to his word my boss helped me. He helped me a lot actually and we ended up chatting more and more. He was different in the evenings, much more relaxed and as he trained me on the procedures and systems. We began to get to know one another and had a laugh chatting about all sorts.

I began to look forward to my overtime and I spent my first increased wage on a big TV for our flat which kept my boyfriend happy and meant I got less grief when I told him I would be working late. That was until I was asked to work one Saturday.

My boss told me we had missed the deadline and had until Monday to complete the job. I had no reason to doubt him so I agreed to help him out. After all he had helped me a lot and I was about to get my promotion so it might be our last overtime together.

My boyfriend went ballistic. A friend of his, from the factory, was leaving to go to Australia and the whole gang had arranged to meet up for lunch on that Saturday and then, 'go on the piss' as he put it for the rest of the day. I told him I didn't know when I would be back or whether I would feel up to joining them after being at work all day but he flew off the handle demanding I join them after work. He had been violent before but this was outrageous behaviour and he scared me so I was actually glad to get to work that Saturday and away from him.

I was told not to come in until eleven o'clock so I got the late train and went for a coffee first. It was a beautiful morning with crisp, clear blue skies and a feeling that Spring was on its way. The trees were budding awaiting their new coat of leaves and the birds were singing away as if summer had already arrived. The coffee shop was on the end of a road sandwiched between two large office blocks. Trees lined the road attempting to add some colour to the grey and glass of the city. They hadn't done their job as they had been bare all winter looking more like twigs than trees but before long they would be full of leaves creating a green plume like a series of umbrellas lining the street.

I finished my coffee and entered the building through the main door. I had never seen the lobby so quiet. The street itself was busy with shoppers heading back and forth towards the shopping area but inside the building it was like a different world. It was empty as if it had been evacuated. Normally the lobby would be full of people dashing this way and that, some carrying books and files others wielding trolleys and carrying cases of work. People would stop there and chat to one another exchanging pleasantries before committing their day to the daily grind.

I made my way to the lift and up to the 16th floor where I was to become office manager. That was to be my floor. I was going to be the boss of the 16th floor. I felt like getting 16 printed onto my jacket like a footballer proud of his number in the squad. I was to become part of a squad, the management squad. A key player, a much needed member of the team and that made me feel proud. My boss had helped me climb the ladder and for that I was grateful but I still had no idea what was to happen next.

At my desk I opened the computer and swiftly realised I was completely alone. Was I early? I thought to myself and then when I logged into the job files from that week I noticed they were completed. I was initially confused as I had been told the deadline had been missed. I sat there for a moment before checking my watch. I wasn't early, it was 11.15am but where was everyone else? I knew my boss would be in so I made my way to his office. I knocked his door and walked straight in.

He was standing with his back to me facing out his enormous window which overlooked the city's business district but before he turned I noticed his meeting table had a tablecloth on it. It was laid out with cutlery and tall slim glasses. There were two place settings and each had a silver dome, like in posh people's houses, covering what must have been food inside.

He turned and exclaimed, 'Congratulations!' and popped the cork on a bottle of champagne. I was shocked and amazed but felt happy. Not just happy but warm inside, from the tips of my toes to the top of my head I was elated, just as it dawned on me that he had done all this for me. That together with my realisation that I had got the job, the one he recommended me for, the one I wanted. I just felt happy. It's hard to describe the feeling because in between those emotions of happiness and feeling that I had achieved something there were the beginnings of a love. Just like those buds on the trees lining the street below opening into the first shoots of Spring outside there, in that room, were the first shoots of a love that I still cherish to this day. The feelings grew from that moment and became part of a solid foundation which today forms the basis of our marriage.

It was magical. We drank champagne and talked, not about work, but about love and life, the universe even. Everything was discussed, even past relationships were brought up. He knew I lived with my boyfriend but we glossed over that. I was happy to be away from him and with this charming, gentle, giant of a man that I now adored. I was being romanced probably for the first time in my life and it was a far cry from my existence before that time.

Perhaps before me I saw the prince I had longed for all my life. The gallant knight to lead me away from where I grew up and take me to a Disney style castle for a happy-ever-after life.

We drank the champagne and then another bottle. I had become relaxed with him before that day but on that day I felt like I had known him forever like we were destined to meet and to get along.

After the lunch we went out together into the city centre. We walked around and chatted. I linked his arm and felt protected by his warmth and physical presence which was no longer threatening to me but felt like it would threaten others. He made me feel safe in his company as well as warm and I wanted to hold on to him forever.

We continued drinking in a wine bar before he said, 'Lets go to the cinema?' but before I could answer he continued, 'come on it'll be fun' and he dragged me across the street. There were only silly movies showing, afternoon matinees but we went anyway and watched a comedy. We were both tipsy and laughed buckets until our sides were too sore to continue.

It was a great day and I felt lifted. I was on a high. I had never felt that way before almost like a feeling that I was special. To him I was perfect. He remarked on everything about me from my hair, my smile, to my body and even my hands. He loved my long nails and said he used to look forward to each day coming into work to see what colour I had painted them. He used to watch my hands as I typed and imagine holding them one day. He was so sweet and when he said that I put my hand in his and we held hands all through the movie. He held my hand and stroked it lovingly with his fingers and in a very sensual way. So sensual in fact I felt moisture in my pants as we left the cinema.

I was feeling more than just happy then and I reckon I was actually feeling quite horny. I was beginning to fall for this man, my boss, in every way, sensually, sexually and romantically. It caught me by surprise but that wasn't the last surprise he had in-store for me.

I didn't get back in time to meet my boyfriend that night and he came home in a rage saying I had showed him up in front of his friends. He was so angry he smashed the mirror above the electric fire and threw the remote control at me. It hit me full whack in my ribs and left me with an awful bruise. I was left feeling sore and I felt ashamed. I knew my mother and his would blame me because I didn't come home or meet him like he wanted. I couldn't tell anyone what was going on in the city and I was so unhappy. I felt so down after being elated as if my world had crashed around me bringing me back to earth with a wallop, literally.

I cried that night as I lay on my bed. I cried hard and uncontrollably as I tried to hold back but the tears just flooded out. I was crying with the pain in my side which was now a dark bruise formed from the initial red and yellow stain after the impact. It hurt but I was also crying for my life, my boss, my prince and the fact that I wanted to be with him. I wanted my prince to ride into the flat on a white horse, lift me up onto his charger and take me away. I wanted the horse to trample my boyfriend, under hoof, as we rode out and on into the sunset.

The reality though was so different. The entrance beside the butcher's was too low for a man on horseback and the steps up too steep; too skinny for a horse and his rider to negotiate so I just lay there weeping. Instead of a rescue my drunken boyfriend came in to apologise and whilst I continued to weep he hitched up my skirt pulled down my pants and entered me. I lay in a crumpled heap on the bed as he thrust inside me whilst I was still crying. This was his way of apologising, by pleasuring himself. I'm sure he thought I would be enjoying it but after I took that job and met my boss I never enjoyed sex with him. We still had sex of course but I never had an orgasm or felt good about it afterwards and this time was no different. It was worse really because I felt sick at him inside me and I lay there motionless, tears lining my cheeks and waited on my prince just hoping to hear his horse, hoping to hear the hooves rattling up the stairs but he never came.

My mother knew I was unhappy as soon as she next saw me but knew also that there was something keeping me alive, something lifting my spirits. She thought, at first, it was my job and my new position that was making me happy. That is until the day she met my boss.

It was coming up to Christmas and I had caught an awful virus. I was so sick I couldn't stay in the flat above the rotten meat and was glad to get away from my useless boyfriend and back to the comfort of my mother's house so she could look after me. I was still with my boyfriend but he wasn't going to care for me and was probably glad of the time alone except for the fact that no-one was making his dinner. I felt awful and spent my days in my P.J's and dressing gown being waited on hand and foot by my mum.

She was great in those situations, always at hand to wipe your brow or stroke your hair and make you feel better. I was glad to be there but missing my work and my boss. We had grown even closer and in my new role we spent a lot of time together. We went to meetings together and I was in and out of his office all the time. We became great friends and even though it was only a few months it felt like we would be together like that always. I imagined us forever working side by side giving each other purpose, giving each other a reason to go to work, to look forward to work even. There was no more overtime but we worked closely together and had lunch together most days. I loved the way he talked and I watched his lips as he did. I loved the way he looked at me with that smile as we chatted together.

I missed that as I lay on the sofa in my mum's front room until one evening when the doorbell went. My mum came into me, 'It's for you shall I bring him in?' she said as I strained my head to look up towards her. 'Who is it?' I said. 'Dunno' her reply as she shrugged her shoulders, 'a man in a suit'. He came in anyway behind her, flowers in one hand and a bag in the other. 'You checking up on me?' came out of my mouth but that's not what I wanted to say. I wanted to say thank you for coming, for caring. Thank you for looking at me every day, smiling at me, making my life happy but instead I came out with that cheeky remark. 'Not at all' he said in his distinguished manner, 'I'm simply here to make sure you are ok and to give you your Christmas presents'. 'I figured you wouldn't be in the rest of this week and I didn't want to miss out on giving you your gifts'. At first I thought everyone must get Christmas gifts. Maybe it was a Secret Santa kinda thing? I think my mum thought the same.

He knelt in front of me and said, 'Hope you get better soon' presenting me with the flowers. 'I'll take them, put them in water' said my mum and as she took them from him she left us alone. I was so embarrassed and yet again my face was getting warmer and beaming below my eyes. It had been so pale before it was just a deep pink this time rather than the red hot face he had given me in my review.

I was a mess, no make up, hair all over the place but he didn't seemed to care and looked at me in the same way as he always did, in that loving sensual way that made me feel warm and wanted. 'I can't stay but I hope you get better for Christmas and hope your enjoy your pressies'. He leant over and kissed my cheek. I so wanted to snog him but my breath was probably disgusting so I kept my mouth shut and smiled. He smelt nice and fresh and I imagined pulling him down on top of me. I wondered if he felt like that about me. Probably not, I thought, not now that he's seen me like this but then again he did come all this way and with flowers. My head was a mess and I was upset that he had to see me at my worst.

When he left my mum said, 'He's after you'. 'Don't be daft' was my reply but she kept on, 'He is I can tell.' Then when I opened my presents it was more than obvious. We had talked before I became ill about our favourites; favourite film, favourite song, perfume, and colour. I was brought back to that moment as I opened the gifts. First a DVD of my favourite film then the CD of my favourite song, then my favourite perfume. 'I told you' barked my mum 'he's after you'. Then I opened the last present. My favourite colour was red and it was a red box. Inside was red tissue paper and on top was red lipstick and red nail polish. I opened the red tissue paper and inside was beautiful and obviously expensive red lingerie. 'What is it?' I could hear my mum say, 'Nothing' I mumbled as I shuffled the box closed, glowing red again in my cheeks.

He had a habit of making me blush.

Chapter Two – Our First Time

That year on Christmas day I sent him a text. I was feeling better and wanted to thank him for the presents. He replied quickly and we spent most of the day chatting by text. It made my day although sometimes I had to hide my phone and it took some time to respond. My phone was on silent so I had to keep checking to see if I had a reply. Sometimes it also took him ages to reply and I wondered what he was doing. He said he was having Christmas dinner in his mum's then going to a party at his friend's house and we kept texting each other late into the evening.

He started asking me to meet him on Boxing Day and for me to get the train into the city. I told him I couldn't as my boyfriend would go crazy but he kept giving me different excuses to get away. Eventually I agreed and I lied to my boyfriend telling him I had to meet a friend from work to go to the sales because she had split with her boyfriend and needed cheering up. He was angry but I told him in front of our family so he couldn't do much complaining. When we got back to our flat he went mad again and we had an almighty row. I felt sick lying, not to him but to my family.

The next morning I got up sharpish jumped in the shower and off I went. I wore the red lingerie my boss had bought me and on the train I painted my nails red which I knew he would like.

He picked me up at the train station in his big fancy black car. It was gleaming as he obviously wanted to impress and did I, with my newly painted red nails. He remarked on them straight away and before long we were holding hands as we drove and chatted about Christmas. It felt like the magic of Christmas had only just arrived for me as he held my hand like he had done that day in the cinema.

We drove for ages into the country. The scenery was beautiful and the hills were capped with snow. He described where we were but I had never seen any of it before. I had lived in and around that area all my life without really venturing out to see the beautiful country around me. I was amazed at the rolling hills but my attention was more on his hand and how it made me feel.

We stopped for lunch in a hotel and as he sat next to me his leg touching mine. I could feel the warmth of him radiating into me through his leg and remembered that time in my review when I wanted his leg to touch mine. We kept holding hands and cuddling until the moment came. He leant in to kiss me, my heart pounded and my blood boiled within me as our lips connected. I felt waves of happiness as his lips tasted exactly as I imagined and his hand rested on my waist just below my breast. His tongue gently pushed inside my mouth. It too was warm and I felt tingly all over as I closed my eyes. Love encircled us like an invisible pink fluffy cloud as we shut out the world and snogged for the first time. I wanted his hand to touch my breast but he was too much of a gentleman and I knew I needed to take the initiative. 'Let's get a room' I suggested to which his gentlemanly reply was, 'Are you sure?' 'I've never been more sure of anything in my life' I said and he went straight over to reception, booked the room and then we made our way into the lift. Already inside was an old retired couple in their late sixties. I'm sure they could feel the tension between us as we passed them and stood to their rear with him behind me, sliding his strong arms around my waist. I took his arms and pulled him closer so he bent over my shoulder looking longingly down to my chest which was heaving as my breath became heavier at the thought of what might happen next. My thoughts were of him and me, him wanting me, feeling me, kissing me again, inside me even.

The old couple couldn't wait to get out but before they did I slid my hands behind me and felt how hard he was, hard with anticipation, hard and ready, hard and wanting, wanting so much to feel my breasts and to see them. I took his bulge in my hands with my perfectly painted nails and began to stroke his trousers making him harder as he held me tighter. The air was filled with a sexual tension that the old couple had probably not felt in years. The lift eventually opened and they got out. Finally we had our chance so I took his hand in mine and slid it up the outside of my top. He took my breast in his hand, in a firm grip and I felt his penis pulsating in my other hand. He was already dying to come but held back as he felt my breast. PING, went the lift as it stopped once more and the doors opened. It was our floor.

We stepped out in trepidation; fear of what would happen next filled our minds as the anticipation of what could happen filled our hearts and underwear. 'Are you sure you want to go to the room?' he asked me once more and he opened the door for me, as ever the gentleman. I walked straight in, strutted in actually, without saying a word and using my actions to answer him. I turned to him as I passed, look into his eyes and smiled taking his hand in mine to lead him in. We entered the room holding hands and still a little nervous with one another, not sure what to expect. I felt anxious at how far we could go especially as we had only just kissed for the first time but our desire for one another could be seen in each others eyes. Then an unexpected knock at the door sent my heart thumping.

Who is it? What's going on? The thoughts raced through my mind. Then my initial fear was, it's my boyfriend! It must be! My face turned white and I felt a sick feeling it the pit of my stomach as he walked over and opened the door. 'Room Service' I heard as the waiter marched in with some champagne that he had sneakily ordered at reception as he booked the room.

The colour returned to my cheeks and I felt relieved.

Champagne again, I thought as I remembered our celebratory lunch in his office and how I felt that day. That then eased the situation and let us both calm down, neither of us too sure about what might happen next but both wanting the same thing…..each other!

As we sipped the champagne and chatted our bodies edged closer on the bed, closer again like before when we were downstairs. I was still a little nervous. Nervous because until then no-one had really taken the lead and I was unsure what to do next but as I stared into his eyes that warm feeling began to burn inside me again. A warm but tender fire flickering and making me want to kiss him again, making me want him, making me want him to be inside me and so I took the lead. I stood up and took his hands pulling him up from the bed and began to kiss him softly as we stood together at the foot of the bed. The kiss was soft and sensual interspersed with the occasional flickering of our tongues on our very wet lips. He then pulled us closer as our bodies writhed together and the champagne began to rush to our heads. Maybe then we are ready. Maybe then we could get closer, closer than before.

He then took the lead and gently spun me round so my back was to him as he brushed my hair aside and kissed my neck. Suddenly we were back in that position as we had been in the lift and I used my hands again, twisting my arms behind me to stroke him and make him hard once more.

That time was different though because we were alone, no old couple holding us back and by that time we were tipsy. We could go further without caring and I think we both felt, at that moment, as if we'd known each other all our lives and getting naked seemed like the natural next step to take. As I began to unbutton his belt he took my top firmly in his hands and lifted it up over my head revealing the sexy red underwear he had bought me and I caught his little smile in the mirror in front of me. His trousers dropped to the floor as he undid my bra strap allowing my new red bra to join his jeans. That was his moment and I knew he had longed to feel my breasts for ages. I too had wanted his hands to hold them in the gentle manner I knew he would. He didn't disappoint and he cupped them like trophies, carefully examining them after months of waiting and wanting to feel them.

His hands were warm and soft and I watched them in the mirror as he played with my boobs. I once again found his hardness with my hands before slipping them inside his boxers. His beautiful skin touching was mine at last. My hands were finally feeling him where I knew he'd imagined them, time and time again, when he talked about them and watched them as I typed in the office.

It couldn't get any better than this, I thought... or could it?

Then it did as he slid his hand inside my new red pants. I'm sure he felt that I was soaking wet, wet and ready, wet and warm after being so cold earlier on the train and when I woke so early to get ready to meet my boss. As we removed our underwear I turned to him now naked and once again we kissed still holding each other tight. This time snogging and snogging harder and more passionately than before. That moment was sheer bliss for me as he held me tight in his strong arms and our naked skin was moulded together in an embrace that I had dreamt of, over and over, since that lunch and our trip to the cinema. I was amazed at his body which was slim but muscular, tight but sexy.

He then gently laid me onto the bed and began to run his hands up and down my naked body. I watched as he took it all in examining every curve with the same close attention he gave to his job. He lay beside me and I too ran my hands over his body enjoying him as he did me. We lay together, feeling each others bodies, holding, touching, groping, grabbing. I was dying for him to be inside me. I couldn't wait and I knew he wanted the same but he held back letting the tension build between us.

He slipped his hand between my legs and they fell open for him, letting him feel all around my inner thigh as he gently brushed past my soaking wet vagina without touching it at first. He would then brush past again and again, more forcefully each time, teasing my clitoris as his fingers skimmed its lips in passing. He then began to rub my clitoris, first gently then hard, like no-one had ever done before. No-one had ever paid that much attention to me or turned me on so much. He found that spot at the top of the clit which is so sensitive and he dug his fingers in, rubbing vigorously.

His fingers slid up and down my wet lips as he rubbed that spot and then slid inside, in and out quickly, teasing me and making me shudder in delight.

He leant in to kiss me as his fingers plunged inside and my body tensed before releasing as he pulled them out. We kissed and kissed as he pleasured me until I couldn't kiss any more. My body was aching as I lay there with waves of intense pleasure coming upwards from between my legs. I lay there letting him finger me and he kissed my neck sending rushes downward to meet the waves of pleasure travelling up. The waves seemed to meet at my chest, filling my breasts with warm beautiful blood and making them sensitive to touch which he did with his mouth. He gently kissed them before licking and then sucking my nipples as if those waves of pleasure were travelling into my breasts and out through my nipples into him. He moaned with pleasure and then I did, unable to hold back I released the pleasure in my groans before grabbing him and holding him close almost digging my nails into his back. I squeezed him tight, my body shuddered and I came.... It was an amazing orgasm that took over my entire body paralysing me and then leaving me with a sensation in my vagina that I had never felt before. It was as if a small vibrator was lodged inside continually releasing wave after wave until at one point I thought it would go on forever.

I wanted to do the same to him, to give him the pleasure he gave me and I wanted to feel him all over and to taste him all over as the waves of orgasm still engulfed my body. So I leant over and begin to play with him. I stroked him again making him even harder before climbing onto him and sliding my breasts down his body and between his legs so he could feel my hard nipples touching him as they glided past his throbbing manhood. I was still wanting, despite my fabulous orgasm. I wanted more, wanting him inside but I knew it would be better to wait so I looked up into his beautiful blue eyes while I began to suck and lick him. I sucked him up and down for only a matter of minutes. He was so excited he came. He was no longer able to hold back after holding back in the lift and then at the end of the bed when my hands had stroked him. After holding back as they stoked him again when we lay on the bed and holding back as we enjoyed each other's naked bodies. It exploded out of him as if it had been held back since the moment we first met, since the handshake in his office.

Finally after all this time, after all our chats and the months of building tension we were lying together, naked on a hotel bed and both feeling great after each experiencing an orgasm with the help of the other.

We lay there relaxed but still not satisfied. Although the initial tension had left us we both knew we wanted more and were now totally relaxed with one another as we lay on the bed. He lay behind me holding me tight with his strong arms. I was moaning gently and smiling. 'What a beautiful smile you have' he said, breaking the silence but I was sure it was the biggest one I had ever displayed on my face. His hands once again drifted towards my breasts. He massaged them, holding me firm in his grip so I couldn't escape, not that I wanted to. The feeling of love filled the air and no longer nervous and totally relaxed I turned to him and said, 'Come inside me?'

He looked at me and without answering slid his body on top of mine as I opened my legs letting him fall between them. That was what we wanted when we arranged to meet that day. That was what we wanted when we were driving in the car, when we kissed downstairs and when we got into the lift. We may have been unsure when we finally arrived in the room but we knew then that this was what we both had wanted all along.

He slid inside me with ease and my head tilted backwards as he penetrated me for the first time. I let out a sound; it was more manly than girly, a groan I would hear time and time again as he would pull back and slide in again and again. Each time harder, pushing my body deep into the bed. My groan became louder with each more forceful thrust inside. He then dropped to one side taking his weight on his left arm to release his right arm so that his right hand could caress my face as he kissed me again while writhing inside me. That moment was special as I realised my prince was inside me and kissing me. He continued to thrust inside me and once again became harder and more forceful. I almost bit my tongue as his free hand grabbed my hair and gently pulled as he penetrated me again and again. His free hand then once again found my breast. That was where he had wanted it for so long, since our first encounter and all that day and so he held it there and kept himself deep inside me. Then as we kissed again he pulled himself fully on top again sliding both his hands under me and grabbing my bum. He pulled me closer digging himself into me, kissing my neck and again my head titled backwards in pleasure as the waves once again flooded up from within me like a tsunami of immense power and emotion.

We both orgasmed again and had made love two more times after that, stopping between sessions to kiss and cuddle, laugh, giggle, order room service and play music. We lay together naked as he gently stroked my skin always looking over me. Keeping me safe but still examining me, taking pictures in his mind of this moment in case it would be his last with me, like this, naked and satisfied.

I ignored my phone which buzzed in my bag, ignoring the consequences of not answering it. Ignoring too my life outside the hotel room and the outside world, opting only for the one we had together. We spent the night together holding one another naked.

The next morning after our night of passion we still lay together for ages until we awoke chatting and looking into each others eyes occasionally kissing and tickling one another. We had slipped under the covers during the night but our naked bodies were still entwined under the sheets. Forgetting again about the outside world our skin slid together and we touched each other everywhere not able to stop touching and caressing until we made love once more.

That time a more gentle morning sex, quick and nice but without an orgasm and I was left once again feeling horny. Even after the day before I still wanted more of this man. I couldn't believe it as I began for the first time to think about the world outside. I thought briefly about my boyfriend and the fact that he had never made me orgasm like that nor had he ever been as tender with me. After sex with him I had no interest in doing it again for a second time let alone a third or fourth.

I eventually rose out of the bed with my body feeling tired but my mind active. I went over to the dressing table and turned on the kettle to make us both a cup of tea.

'Fancy a cuppa?' I said as I stood there naked in front of my boss. 'Yes please' his reply with manners. Always the gentleman I thought until I saw his eyes. The stare followed me as he watched me and once again took in my body and its curves as if video taping me with his memory. His stare made me feel even more horny as it appeared sexy and almost dirty. I could tell he would be rising again getting hard once more and ready soon to pleasure me all over again.

I walked over to him and watched as his eyes as they examined my breasts again in detail. I knew him by then and I knew that look as I sat on the bed setting his cup of tea on the bedside cabinet. As I sipped my tea before putting it down beside his I slipped my cool hand under the covers. It was very warm under the duvet so the shock of my colder hand made him wince arching his back before I grabbed him letting all the heat escape from him and into my hand. I sat there holding his penis and looking into his eyes. I gently caressed it until it was rock hard again before yanking it hard to pull him forward making him rise from the bed. I led him by his penis into the bathroom, still holding him tight as it began to pulsate.

We both knew we were heading for the shower so that once again we could caress one another.

As I leant in to turn the shower on I turned him on too and he grabbed my bum and I giggled, giddy with anticipation and pleasure. Leaning back into him I felt his hands drift once again to my ample bosom before pulling me tight to feel his warm front against my cool back and then I stepped into the shower. At first he watched me once again examining me in detail as I pulled my hair back under the water. He seemed amazed, taken aback even, at my beauty and my body, amazed and unbelieving that he had been so lucky to, only yesterday be inside me for the first time and to have finally won the opportunity to spend this time with me.

He then stepped inside.

By then I had lathered my body with the soap so when he pulled me to him my breasts slipped against his chest and I slid my hands down to hold him again, gently stroking him up and down in my soapy hands. His hands slid all over me finding my bum then up my sides and then again briefly onto my breasts before taking my face in my hands and saying, 'Thank-you for this'. My hands continued again to slide up and down his hard shaft in a soapy lather as I smiled in recognition.

He held my face as he kissed me and licked my mouth swirling his tongue around mine. My stroking began to pull him forward and he became harder in my hands until without warning he pulled me out of the water and turned me round pushing me forward and holding my shoulders as he bent me over into my favourite position, doggy style and it was the prefect end to our encounter. My hands were resting on the wet but still cold tiles and for a second he seemed be fixated once again on them and on my red nails until this seemed to raise his level of excitement and he pushed himself hard inside me from behind. My usual moan became more like a yell and inside he wriggled around twisting his pelvis before thrusting harder and harder whilst sliding his hands all over my body grabbing at my breasts. He banged and banged at me and my noises became much more excitable, much more than the night before. I was loving it and he could tell. He knew me, he knew what I liked and his hand finally found its way to mine pressing against it as it gripped the tiles. His fingers slid in between mine and I gripped his hand hard as we came together and held that position so I could feel him pump into me.

Sadly it all had to end and it did abruptly when I finally picked up my phone after getting dressed. 19 missed calls and countless messages awaited me. I listened to my voicemail and quickly erased the expected irate messages from my boyfriend until I began to hear worry in his voice and then messages from my family, my mum, my sisters. They were worried about me and didn't know what had happened to me. I felt guilty; sick even, as the real world came crashing into that hotel room. The love that had once filled the air disappeared and the passion that was in my life seemed so far in the past as that dark day poured into the room.

He left me back to the train station and we kissed before I left to get my train. We didn't say much and he knew what was in store for me. We wouldn't see each other again until the New Year when we went to work but we promised to text. I didn't keep my promise because there was a lot going on at my end. Fights and arguments were the order of the day with everyone on my case. I was so sad, so lonely and unable to fight back as it seemed they were all against me. All on his side because they didn't understand and I couldn't tell them the truth in case they hated me more.

I was alone and unable to cope anymore so I bit the bullet and I dumped my boyfriend. My friends were his friends, really, so they were all against me and against the split. My family didn't understand and questioned me over and over again, 'Why? Why?' but I couldn't explain.

My mum knew though, I could see it in her eyes and she was the only one that didn't badger me with questions. She knew where I was on Boxing Night and why I was so upset. She knew deep down I was in love and as she too had been in love with my father so she knew the pain in my heart as it ached for my man, my prince, my boss.

I didn't answer his texts and he then became worried himself, sending me even more questions. The pressure was intense and unbearable. On New Year's Eve I went to a party with my so called friends. My ex was there even though they promised he wouldn't be. He spent the night pleading with me for a kiss at midnight, asking me to go back with him, telling me how he would change, how things would be different and I very nearly agreed until 11.52pm that night when I received a text from my boss which simply read;

I love you

That was exactly what I needed, perfect timing as usual. My heart melted inside but I remained hard nosed while my friends tried to resolve things with me and my ex. I knew the New Year would be great. I wanted to be with my boss and I was sure he wanted to be with me. I just had to get through the next few days until I got back to work and he would be there on his white horse, waiting for me. I was convinced of it and that got me through.

I couldn't have been so wrong!

Sure enough when I got back to work he was there, in his suit. No white horse but immaculately dressed as usual. I asked him to join me for lunch so I could fill him in on all my troubles and we decided to leave the building in order to talk privately.

I poured my heart out to him over a tuna pasta salad and a smoothie, tears rolling down my cheeks as I confessed my love and my need for him to remove me from my awful predicament but his expression was different. His eyes were glazed, no longer fixed in that stare. His body language was stand-offish as he sat upright in his seat. I knew something was wrong but was not prepared for what happened next.

Chapter Three – Getting Together Was Complicated

He told me he was married!

I couldn't believe it. My tears became floods and I was so glad we had left the building for lunch. People stared at me (thankfully strangers) as my shoulders shook and I cried hard. He put his hand onto mine to consol me but I pulled it away. How could he do this to me? I had turned my back on my friends and family and wanted nothing more than to be with him. I gave up my boyfriend and now had no-where to live.

I couldn't move back in with my family, not at my age, I had flown the nest and I couldn't cope with the thought of returning there permanently.

His usually charming patter was broken as he stumbled through his feeble explanation stating that I had a boyfriend and that somehow, just because I didn't know about his wife, it was still the same thing. He continued on as I watched his lips mouth the words. The same lips that had first attracted me to him were delivering daggers into my heart with every word, telling me that he loved me and that he would leave her for me. I didn't believe him, why didn't he tell me before? I never asked but it kept reverberating in my mind. It was a pitiful excuse and it wouldn't wash and so I stormed out of the place straight across to the office, grabbed my bag and left, leaving work and heading home. I was in too much of a state to return to work. He was the boss and it was his fault so he could explain to his seniors why his precious office manager was no-where to be seen.

That journey home on the train seemed to drag on forever. I wanted to be at home with my mum, in the comfort of the house I grew up in and locked away from the real world. I sat on the train as it seemed to labour along stopping at every station and the rain trickled along the window in lines. I put on my iPod and turned the volume up high. I didn't care if anyone could hear it I just wanted to block out the world.

The songs that kept coming on shuffle were all slow and seemed to bring me down further into the depths of my despair. I shivered with cold as if my heart had given up pumping warm blood and my finger tips were freezing. I held my hands to my face and blew onto them but only cold air came out and it seemed I had left all my heat behind in that café. I wanted my boss to hold me again in his arms and fill me with the warmth we shared on Boxing Day.

I remember then listening to Joy Division and an old track I had downloaded after seeing it in a movie. I played it over and over again, *'Love will tear us apart'*, as I cried on the train, trying desperately to hold back the tears from all the prying eyes around me.

That night after work he again came to my mum's. When the door knocked I knew it was him. At first I refused to talk to him but he wouldn't leave so I agreed to go with him. I had been so upset when I got home that I had told my mum everything. I broke down in floods of tears and recalled the whole thing to her. I told her everything that happened; from the review, my overtime, my promotion, our lunch and time at the cinema right up to Boxing Day (without giving her the gory details).

She was understandably worried when I agreed to leave with him but a part of her knew he was a nice man and when we had spoken about him earlier she was able to offer his side while I wailed at her, 'It cant have been easy for him either' she said and things to that effect. My mother would never have stuck up for him if she had any doubts about his intentions. She had only met him once but she was always good judge of character.

Despite that though she was nervous when I left with him. 'Leave your mobile on', she shouted after me as I got into his shiny, black motor.

He drove, he talked and I listened. For once it was him telling me about his life and I wondered had I ever given him the chance before, to speak or to tell me all of this. We drove for ages until he finally pulled up at the side of the road. It was in the countryside and it was pitch black outside, as if we were inside a thick black cloud with no lights or people it seemed, for miles around. Just us two back once again in that world we had before, just us.

He said, 'Come here' and beckoned me to sit on his knee. I crawled across and sat on his knee as he wrapped his arms around me. I felt like a little girl sitting in his lap but I felt safe, warm and happy again. It was just what I needed and what I had wanted before when I sat freezing on the train. His warmth filled me once again as he held me and told me how he felt about me. He told me that as long as I felt the same and wanted the same things, he would go straight home and end it with his wife.

He told me he wanted to settle down and have kids one day and we both shared our thoughts on life and the future. Eventually we kissed; it wasn't a sexy snog but a long, lingering, loving kiss as if the lust we once shared had evolved into this love.

True to his word he left her. It was messy with a lot of crying and shouting, even from her family. They all seemed shocked and upset. Even his own mother tried to talk him out of it, as did his friends. None of them knew me and it annoyed me that they did this without even having met me but I stayed out of it.

Before long though I had met his friends and his family and they all accepted me into their fold. They could see how he loved me and how we were together and knew it was the right decision for him and for us.

Chapter Four — Married Life

Our wedding day was amazing. All our friends and family all together and everyone there just for us. It is such a special day in everyone's life and mine was the happiest day, so happy in fact I got tipsy before the ceremony.

Everyone was giving me glasses of champagne while I was getting ready even before I left my mum's house. My sisters and my aunties were there all guzzling the stuff but taking breaks as they got their make-up or hair done. I on the other hand was last to get everything done so I had lots more than everyone else. The hairdresser and make up girls all came to my mum's as the cars were picking us up from there.

I remember walking down the stairs with mum at the bottom, finally ready and finally able to make my way to the church. I nearly fell down the stairs I was so tipsy but I was also calm, not nervous at all. My mum on the other hand was going through so many cigarettes she looked like a woman shaped chimney as she puffed away at her front door. I remember her stinking of smoke in the car as we approached the hotel. We got married in a civil ceremony in the hotel and my husband and the boys had stayed there the night before so that morning before I arrived they too had enjoyed a few drinks at the bar.

The ceremony itself was short but very sweet and we had a laugh both being tipsy especially as I couldn't get his ring on. I thought I was seeing too many fingers as I swayed after attempting to stand there for what seemed like ages but was only a short while.

They say your wedding night should be special but ours wasn't exactly that. We had a great day but by the evening I was so drunk and tired that I crashed on the bed and fell asleep, fully clothed, in my wedding dress with all the clips still holding up my hair. When I woke the next morning the bones in my dress had dug into me creating deep red tracks on my skin and my head was so sore with my hair still pinned back. It took my husband over half an hour to remove all the clips from my hair and ease the pain in my head.

We didn't consummate the marriage until we arrived at our honeymoon destination. It was a beach resort in the Caribbean and we spent two weeks lazing around and making love over and over again. Making up for the wedding night we were at it like rabbits, sometimes in the morning, sometimes in the afternoon and also at night.

Our married life was probably not much different than most. At first we spent a lot of time together and had sex all the time. We remained professional when at the office but I remember dying to finish work and get home to be with him privately and I know it was the same for him, watching the clock tick slowly to 5pm so we could race home to embrace. We travelled separately most days as our hours differed depending on meetings and deadlines but the feeling of being home first waiting on him was great. Just knowing he would be home soon to kiss me, embrace me, service me even. I couldn't wait and when I heard the door I would often get goose-bumps.

It was a far cry from my old life, trudging home in the rain then slaving over his dinner and watching him wolf it down in front of the telly. My life was exciting and my husband made it complete. We would always kiss each other each morning as we said goodbye finding it so hard to part and then a huge hug and long lingering kiss would say hello again each night as if we had not seen each other that day at all.

We couldn't wait to go to bed each night and sometimes we didn't make it that far ending up having sex on the sofa or on the living room floor and even on occasion, at the weekends after a bottle of wine, we would curl up together on the sofa after making love and fall asleep naked and knowing we would have sex again when we woke the following day.

He was a great cook and loved to prepare dinner while I watched and chatted about the day. Many a time we would sip wine and dinner became part of the evening rather than a chore. He would often come home and say I've booked a table and we would dine out, again sweeping me off my feet with his spontaneity and zest for life.

It was a great time in both our lives when we first got married and moved in together but before long it became less intense. When he worked very late he came home too tired and we no longer had sex every night. Before too long it became a weekend thing that was almost planned or necessary and that made it feel less appealing to me.

The spontaneous nights out became planned and life became routine. The sex we had was good, great sometimes but the build up was gone and the desire and excitement was flat. The feeling afterwards was the same though, that never changed. I loved him and I loved him inside me. I felt close to him when we made love but that's what it became, making love. We never had wild rampant sex in fact we didn't even snog anymore. We kissed but not for long periods, not like those first evenings when we would snog on the sofa for hours while he groped me and we undressed each other.

By then we went to bed and although sometimes we would make love most nights we went to bed to sleep and bed became the place of rest rather than the place where we had always became entwined.

Chapter Five – Porn

Before long routine had set in and although we loved each other dearly the passion was no longer there. Our relationship was built on a mutual understanding grounded by a deep love for one another but the lust was lacking on both parts. We still enjoyed nights out and having friends round but the mundane drudgery of life seemed to tick by without any real excitement being interjected into the daily grind.

My husband was no longer working in the place where had met and had moved on to a bigger, better job. We no longer saw each other during the day but still chatted each day on the phone, still do in fact.

My husband was away a lot during the week on business trips, mostly one night at a time and I found myself travelling back to stay at my mum's rather than be alone in the city. I no longer minded going there as it was like a sanctuary rather than a retreat. I was able to go back safe in the knowledge that my life was elsewhere and that I could leave and go back to it anytime. It became a comfort going there, almost like going home.

That was until one Thursday evening when I was

staying behind to achieve a deadline; he was working in London and wouldn't be back to the Friday. It would be too late to go to mum's after work so instead I went home. I chatted to my husband on the phone before saying goodnight but I couldn't sleep; I hated being there alone and never felt safe without him there. I found myself flicking channels on the TV but found nothing of interest although kept it on anyway to drown out the silence.

I decided to log onto the computer and browse the net. Shopping pages mostly interested me, latest fashions, what the celebs were wearing, usual girlie sites. I made a typing error on Google and a name I didn't recognise appeared. I followed the link to the page and was shocked with what I found. It was password protected but for some reason the password was stored on the computer so it opened automatically. I couldn't believe my eyes it was filth, porn in fact and video clips of people having sex! I knew it was my husband's site and his password as only he and I used the computer. I was upset and angry and then afraid. I was afraid that if he had this and was hiding it from me, could he, or was he, hiding anything else? Of course I had to find this when he was away, staying away in a hotel and so my mind wandered into a jealous haze. Perhaps he was meeting someone? I was thinking, another woman?!

Everyone told me it wouldn't last. He was married when we first had sex and we were married now so was it possible he was doing it all over again and with another woman? My jealously clouded my vision and judgement. I was already appalled that my husband was watching porn; after all I was better looking than the girls on that site! I was still there though in front on the screen, transfixed on it and as I sifted through all the clips he had downloaded none of them interested me just made me ill as the jealous rage built up inside me.

I watched on and saw my husband in the clips, imagining him with each different woman, doing what they were doing and then doing it right there and then, thinking to myself that I was at home, his naive wife, sleeping in our bed while he was doing these things to some other woman.

The noises coming from the computer added fuel to my clouded visions and my husband had sex with each of the women I saw before me and although I couldn't turn away I felt the hurt and betrayal of a man, who in my eyes, had committed adultery.

I seethed with rage but didn't ring him. I didn't even call him the next morning after that torturous night. I didn't ring him at lunchtime and he didn't ring me. I knew he was cheating on me and his lack of calls confirmed it. Just as I had not answered my phone when I cheated with him he too was not using his phone, staying away from the real world with some other woman, some tart!

Eventually he rang as he checked in at the airport. I exploded at him over the phone letting rip about what I had found and immediately firing accusations at him. I ranted as he checked in his bags. In fact I continued all the way to the departure gates. I screamed the words

DIVORCE and SELL THIS HOUSE and god knows what else at him, not letting him get a word in reply.

Eventually the rant turned into a conversation as he remained calm throughout. His tone eased the tension and his forceful manner ended the conversation with, 'I can't talk now I have to get on the plane' and 'we will discuss this when I get home.'

I would've packed my bags had I believed in my heart he was playing away but in my head my bags were already packed, the house was up for sale and the solicitors were instructed.

That night we drank wine and shouted at each other. It wasn't like the rows I had with my last boyfriend. Yes he got angry, very angry at times but I never felt threatened. We screamed at each other. I think I actually enjoyed it and I know now it was long overdue.

It was unhealthy for him to hide his watching of porn but that's all it was in the end. He was getting off on it and fantasised about me and him getting involved in some of the activities he watched. He knew I was better looking than the women he watched and he didn't watch it to see naked women but rather to watch the act they carried out and to imagine him and I doing the same. He admitted that sometimes he even imagined the bloke in the act doing it with me and yes he sometimes imagined him with the girl but it was a fantasy and something to give him a release or to start him off while he masturbated.

The conversation needed to continue and we went

away that weekend and stayed in a hotel near the sea. We went for long walks and talked and talked, always about sex and everything connected to it. He was open with me about masturbating, how and when he did it and how he longed for me to do it to him.

He told me about his desires and sexual fantasies and that he would love to watch me and another man. A lot of what he said shocked me but I have to say aroused me also. I felt myself getting wet as he talked about another man touching me, feeling me, fucking me, whilst he knew in the end I was his and would be coming back to him at the end of it. I imagined the men in the clips I saw fucking me as I watched his lips say the words.

We talked more over lunch and then dinner. I got more and more turned on by his words. Getting inside his head and his mind was an insight, not just into a man, I thought I already knew but into the mind of a now married man and into, what could be the mind of many more married men. Men who might fantasise and masturbate about their desires without ever telling a soul. Men who might love their wives but still lust after other women or scenarios, be it with their wife or other people's wives.

With men it seemed no strings attached sex was better than the complication of a relationship. Whereas the bond and the tie was what women needed to be able to have sex with others. Was that the problem? Was that society's problem? Was that why many marriages failed? These thoughts raced through my mind as I began to be brainwashed by the simplicity of having sex with others whilst being married to my man.

I began to convince myself that this was right and what everyone needed. To have sex with other people and enjoy life, enjoying the freedom to roam without roaming, to explore whilst staying at home, to sow your wild oats while staying firmly rooted to you soul mate. It seemed exciting and we talked about letting each other have sex with someone else and watching, joining in even. We then discussed threesomes but never the practicalities of how you would go about something like that.

He created a hunger in me, a hunger that I thought I had already fulfilled. A desire I thought was over, a need to find out more and to see how the porn affected him. I wanted to watch him watch porn and that night in our hotel room that's exactly what I did.

I fulfilled his fantasy as I wanked him off while we watched porn together. He told me that he had always wanted this but didn't know how or when to approach it with me he told me how he found the website and longed to tell me about it so that I could enjoy it with him. That's why he said he didn't attempt to hide it or the password, knowing, hoping, one day I would come across it. He couldn't, however find the right moment or the right time to tell me and as time went on and he saw more and more it felt like he could never tell me as if it would be more like coming clean than telling me about his discovery.

It was out in the open now and for him that was great but for me it was the beginning. The beginning of a journey of intense sexual pleasure and desire. One that began in that hotel room as I got wetter and wetter and I rubbed my hand up and down his shaft before kneeling in front of him and giving him a blow job. The porn was still on in the background and continued to excite me as I recognised the noises coming from the hotel TV.

We had sex that night, again and again just like we had the first time we met. It was more familiar and we didn't need to explore each others bodies as much but it was just as intense, if not more so.

We talked openly about it after that and it spiced up our sex life. I had been sexually active a lot when I was younger and was no prude but my life had veered away from sex as a means of pleasure or excitement and it had become more of a bond for a loving couple to enjoy.

That all changed after I discovered the porn on his computer and from then on my view of sex and sexual acts changed.

My husband made me a DVD of his favourite clips and I myself would masturbate as I watched it when I found myself alone. I bought myself a vibrator and enjoyed watching the clips myself. I didn't keep it from him and we were open about all of it. He masturbated more than me, a lot more but then the pleasure I got from the vibrator was not that good.

It made me orgasm but it was short lived, over too quick. I knew what I needed and that was to have sex with a stranger. I was never interested in the lesbians on the DVD only the men and now the thought of being fucked by a stranger consumed me.

Before long the discussions turned once again to having a threesome.

Chapter Six – Threesome

I agreed to the threesome with another girl but laid down some ground rules first. If he was going to shag this girl it had to be doggy style, I didn't want her looking at him when he was inside her and I certainly didn't want him kissing her while he fucked her. If he was going to kiss anyone when he was inside her it had to be me. He happily agreed and made contact with her to tell her the rules.

We decided it would be best to have a small private party at our house. Just the three of us in fact. I was a bit wary of this because I knew this girl. She was a friend of a friend and a regular at our house. My husband and her both enjoyed each others company so much I was afraid of feeling like a gooseberry in my own house and with my own husband but it wasn't like that as they were both careful to include me and it was a surprisingly pleasant evening.

When she arrived I was sitting on the sofa making sure I was in the middle so that they would have to sit either side. I had seen them kissing before on the lips, but never snogging. We often kissed friends saying hello or goodbye and were both comfortable with it so

I wondered how I would feel. He met her at the door took her coat and followed her in. She arrived first into the living room wearing a low cut pink top showing off her cleavage and of course no bra.

She often came to our house without one and I thought she did this to tease my husband. I must say, however, that night I looked at her tits and thought, they look very nice. She was wearing a short skirt also pink. I hadn't dressed for the occasion and was wearing my usual t-shirt and jeans. I wasn't wearing a bra either but I rarely did around the house and it was MY house!

My husband was just wearing a shirt and jeans but it was a nice black shirt and I thought he looked smart. She sat on my left and immediately started chatting. She was like an energiser bunny as she talked and talked so quickly I was amazed at how much she had to say and how fast she was saying it. I watched her lips as she talked and could see the attraction my husband had for her. She had a gorgeous face and a fit body, taller than me with longer legs. Her breasts were nice and pert but not as big as mine. He skin was paler and she had lovely hands. My husband, as you know, loves hands especially long nails and hers were perfect with light pink nail polish. She looked lovely, sweet even and as she rabbited on I wasn't really listening but when my husband arrived with the drinks he kissed her as he gave her the wine glass. I wasn't expecting it and as he pulled away he went back again. I certainly wasn't expecting that!

They were both snogging in front of me and I could tell she loved it, not because she had my man but because it was him, she really liked him. Strangely that made it easier and as I watched them I have to admit I got a little turned on but then he slid his hand inside her top and started to grope her tit. I was taken aback. I wasn't ready. He was supposed to sit beside me! What about me? I thought, I'm still here ya know! but they didn't stop snogging and what happened next shocked me even more.

She stood up, her tongue still inside my husbands mouth, his hand still inside her dress feeling her wildly. He was now upright again as they continued kissing. I'm not having this, I thought but before I said anything his hand came out to me and I put mine into his. He pulled me up off the sofa and put my hand onto her breast through her dress. She turned away from him and looked right into my eyes before leaning forward. What's going on I thought as her lips touched mine and she began to kiss me. It was nice, like a man but softer, kinder, nicer almost. I couldn't help but kiss her back until our tongues were now entwined like his and hers had been just moments before. My left hand was still on her tit but I just didn't feel comfortable with it there and didn't know what to do with it.

As she kissed me she took my t-shirt in her grip and pulled it up over my head exposing my bare breasts. It wasn't long before my husband who was standing behind me had his hands on them.

I was enjoying this now sandwiched between the pair of them and she was enjoying me too. My husband took off my jeans while still behind me letting the girl slide her hands inside my pants. She was kissing my neck now in all the right places sending shivers down my spine. Now she was kissing my breasts I couldn't believe that a girl was licking and sucking my nipples as she fiddled with my pussy inside my pants. My husband kindly removed my pants leaving me naked in front of this girl. I knew her but not that well! Her hands moved over my body in a lovely way and my husband was no longer behind me. I could see him behind her as she continued to suck and tease my nipples. He didn't look at me as he unzipped her top and began undressing her. She stopped sucking me and turned to him as her top feel to the floor. His hands were all over her all over her tits. I wanted to touch them and to suck them as she had done to mine and so I did. I began feeling her tits, feeling his hands feeling her tits, rubbing and caressing each others hands as well as her nipples as she leant her head back to kiss him and he buried his tongue deep into her mouth. I was so horny.

She eventually turned around to face him and began to undress him unbuttoning his shirt and sliding her perfect little hands inside and all over his body. I felt compelled to touch her, to grope her bum as I could see him struggling with his jeans.

I wanted to help him but her bum was so smooth in my hands that I couldn't let go rubbing and pinching it in my hands. She turned to me now wrapping her arms around my head still with her back to me pulling me forward and into her back my nipples touching her back as she took my hands and placed them between her legs. She leant back to kiss me once again and we enjoyed a snog as my hands rubbed between her legs.

Her hands were now on my husband, feeling his balls and cock. Her lovely little perfectly manicured hands were all over my husbands cock while my fingers were toying with her pussy.

I got a sudden dose of reality and pulled my hands away. I wasn't sure I wanted to go on and as I stepped back I watched them rubbing against one another almost fucking in front of me. I realised that it turned me on. I was so horny watching them. I wasn't happy with my fingers inside her but I liked watching them for a short time anyway. Eventually though enough was enough I was getting horny and I wanted my husband so I walked past them and grabbed his hand pulling them apart and said, 'Let's go upstairs'.

We all walked naked up the stairs with me leading the way. I wondered who my husband would take first. Who he would want but I in my mind I knew I wanted to see him and watch him as he fucked her so I took the lead, 'Why don't you get on the bed?' I said to her and she did. She immediately got onto all fours just as planned; just as the rules had stated. My husband followed her but before he mounted her I came behind him and grabbed his penis tight in my hand from behind his back. He turned to kiss me with his hands on her cheeks and I remembered her soft cheeks as I watched him caressing them and enjoyed him snogging me. Will I let him inside her? I thought to myself before, fuck it, yes, I want him in and I guided him over to her.

He entered her with ease whilst still kissing me. I was running my hands all over him as his butt clenched and he bucked and bucked at her. I was so fucking horny I couldn't stop kissing him, lashing my tongue in and out in the knowledge he was inside her. I didn't want him to stop kissing me but eventually he turned and pulled out grabbing at her tits as he came all over her back. I was pleased he didn't come inside her and was saving himself for me. I thought about our usual sex, him on top, me below but this time I wanted it to be different and as she turned around to face him I put myself between them. I didn't want her gazing into his eyes. I wanted her to see me to remind her I was there and that he was mine. I got into her position all fours in front of my husband with her below me.

He then bucked hard into me, doggy style, in deep the way I liked it. I loved it, loved feeling his hands enjoying my bum, my body and my breasts but I was surprised by the girl below me. She lay on the bed below me, not looking to catch his eye but looking to catch mine! Wanting me! She started feeling me again all over lifting her head to kiss that spot again in my neck. This was heaven, my husband deep inside while this beautiful girl tickled and teased me, plucking my nipples and licking my neck.

Her hands then ran down my body until in between my legs and began rubbing me just at the perfect spot. I could feel my husband penetrating me as she rubbed the top of my clitoris. It was fantastic! One of the best orgasms ever! My body shuddered as I came like hundreds of tiny speeding cars had raced through my blood, growing in size in my veins, bursting through my body while she rubbed my clit and he banged at me from behind. Her teeth gently nibbled my nipples and I cannot tell you how good that felt until I suddenly became too tender. There was just too much sensation everywhere. It was almost like the ultimate high all over my body and I couldn't take any more.

Thankfully my husband came inside me and I fell onto the girl as he fell onto me and we lay in a tangled mess of naked limbs gently touching each other untill I fell asleep.

I'm sure my husband fucked her again that night, maybe more than once but I didn't care. I realised that night how watching him with someone could be a turn on. I realised that I didn't have to be jealous of her wanting him because she wanted me too. I didn't have to be jealous of him wanting her because I was there with him experiencing her with him. In fact I too was getting an ultimately pleasurable experience at the same time.

Chapter Seven — Swinging

We became more and more open about our sexual fantasies and desires after the threesome and I became more relaxed about my husband's desire to have sex with other women. I realised it was not out of love for another but more of an attraction that might fester if not satisfied. Why not? I thought. Why can't people enjoy each other without having to run off with them? After all when I was younger I was no angel, in fact I would have considered myself adventurous. That side of me didn't have to die just because I was married, did it?

I enjoyed watching porn and there were things I wanted to try myself. I wanted once more for men to chase after me like they did when I was younger and I began to come around to the idea of swinging. The idea being that we would go to a party, swap partners and then go home together as a married couple. No harm in that, I thought.

It wasn't that easy though. We were young and at most parties the other couples were a lot older and had been with each other many times before. We were in demand because our bodies were tight and fresh. My husband

and I had a nickname for them, wrinklies! When we arrived we would whisper to one another, 'Too many wrinklies here', make our excuses and then leave. Occasionally we would stumble across some younger swingers and have a laugh with them. First timers, they would be (most of them) and sometimes not even ready for the next step. Sometimes their spouses would not be as ready as them and I can recall one party when my husband and I swapped partners and my guy was a bit too eager to get me upstairs. So much so he stopped me on the stairs and started kissing my neck as he put his hand up my skirt. I could tell it would be rushed sex but we never made it to the bedroom as his wife became irritated with him and they had a row and then left. My husband was never sure if it was him that put her off but I knew it was his wide eyes when he saw me. That together with the thoughts, in her head, that he might think of me when they next had sex or perhaps even time and time again after our encounter.

I suppose that was always the problem. It was difficult to get two couples where all four people would be happy to swap and I thought, at first, that you need to want to be with someone to go to bed with them. Then as I felt I was becoming less and less fussy my husband was finding it harder and harder to find someone he was happy to bed.

This being the case we mostly stayed away from those types of parties where you pick a name from a hat and just get anyone. That said we did become known in the circuit and amongst other swingers but found it better to have our own parties where we could invite who we wanted or pick another couple to spend time with together.

We were already famous with our friends for having wild parties at our house so adding potential swingers to the mix just spiced things up and we quickly became known as a new type of swinger who mixed young single people in with young married and living-together couples for sexual but no-strings-attached fun.

This involved organising threesomes for friends as well as foursomes for ourselves and strangely, although we talked about it a lot, we never managed a threesome with my husband and I along with another bloke but we did come close once.

It was a stormy night and we were invited to a swinger's house out in the country (as most of them are). It took us some time to find it as there were a lot of minor roads and we had taken the wrong turn on a couple of occasions.

The roads had large potholes filled with muddy water and the rain was coming down in sheets almost attacking the car with venom as it lashed against the windscreen. I asked my husband was it worth it but we continued on. When we finally arrived it was obvious why it was so hard to find. It was an old farmhouse surrounded on all sides by tall trees with barely any lights on.

We were able to drive up to the front door and were surprised at the lack of cars. We ran from the car, coats over our heads, towards the front door. I remember soaking my legs as the splashes of water hit the backs of them as I ran.

The door was opened promptly by an older gentleman with a grey moustache. He was finely dressed in a dinner jacket and at first I though he was the butler.

'Come in come in, dreadful weather', he remarked as he took our coats and hung them gently onto a rack of hooks behind the door. I remember seeing some other coats but also a load of empty pegs prompting me to question, 'Are we early?'

'No, no,' he said 'not many willing to come out in that weather' he continued, 'just a few of us tonight, come through. Would you like a drink?'

He led us into what looked like the sitting room which was warmed by a large open fire crackling in its centre. The orange glow was the only light in the room as I looked around, not noticing at first what was on the sofa in the corner.

We had accepted his offer of whiskey after he had answered his question himself. My husband had said to make his a small one so he had the option to drive away if required. As we walked into the room it became apparent we weren't alone and although the light was dim my eyes began to focus on the sofa in the corner.

At first it looked like a pile of severed limbs seeming not to belong to anyone in particular but as my eyes became accustomed to the night I realised it was two naked women on top of a man. The man seemed also to be of the same age as our butler and I wondered if he was the owner.

We were handed the whiskies and asked to sit down as the man began chatting completely oblivious, it seemed, to the acts being carried out at the other side of the room.

As we chatted it became apparent that our butler was in fact the owner and that he had invited us both there to ask if he could have sex with me?

I was too busy concentrating on the three naked bodies at first to realise and I saw one women climb onto the man's lap while the other kissed him. The one in his lap began bouncing up and down and leaning backwards as she was riding him. They weren't quiet either, giggling and moaning and causing enough of a distraction for me not to pay attention to the man or my husband and their conversation.

It seemed that my husband had agreed, as long as it was ok with me and as long as he could be there and could watch. He told me afterwards that he wanted to make sure I was safe rather than watch for pleasure but found himself getting very aroused by it and still masturbates about it to this very day.

Although the whole thing started off as a creepy scene from a horror film the sexual acts being performed made me horny and the noises the women made turned me on more. When my husband questioned him about the three in the corner he said he enjoyed watching people having sex and had paid two prostitutes to have sex with a friend while he watched. This was, he said, mainly because he didn't think we would turn up due to the weather. He further sated that having my husband watch was also a personal pleasure of his and that he was extremely grateful that we had accepted his request in such a manner.

We all went upstairs and into a bedroom with an old four poster bed. The décor was old fashioned but quaint and all the wood was a dark mahogany. Although it looked old and perhaps dated it seemed expensive and well maintained for a man living on his own.

I was wearing a jade green dress and he asked my husband to remove it while he himself got undressed and lay on the bed. He watched as my husband slowly removed my dress and gently caressed the sensual parts of my body with his hands as he brushed past. I was tingling all over as I watched the man in front of me masturbate.

He kept playing with himself as my husband groped me. My hubby could never resist grabbing my naked breasts and so as he did I turned to snog him. We kissed while he felt me up and rubbed between my legs. His magic fingers rubbed and fingered me, making me very wet.

I was so horny and the man too was gagging for it. My husband walked around to my side, took my hand, walked me over to the bed and set me down beside the naked man who was still feeling himself. My husband then reached into his pocket and took out a condom which he handed to me. I opened the wrapper and leaned over to the man who took his hands away immediately and grabbed my breasts as I rolled the condom on. I pulled myself onto the bed and over on top of the man as his hard hands rubbed my legs and body. He leaned forward putting his face between my boobs then licked them before sucking hard on my nipples. I sat on top of him and took his cock in my hand sliding it into me. I bounced up and down on him and leant back just like the girl had done downstairs. I then remember looking over at my husband who was holding his cock in his hand.

He winked at me before I leant forward again placing my hands on the man's chest and rubbing his hairs as he fondled me. When his hands were on my legs I felt movement behind me and then my husband's hands on my breasts as he massaged them from behind sending the man wild with excitement as he watched him feel me. I turned to my husband and snogged him again as the man bucked wildly up into the air firing me up and down like a wild stallion. As he lunged upward for a final time he came into his condom. My husband was holding me and kissing me whilst this man was still inside me.

Later that night my husband and I made our excuses and went home and although we arrived home late we had fantastic sex for ages and well into the dawn of the following day.

Chapter Eight – Keys In A Bowl

We did, however, continue to try to swing on the circuit (so to speak) and found that once word got around we were invited to all sorts of parties. On some occasions people would travel from other countries to take part in organised swinging events but we tended to stay local and near us was a whole fraternity of swingers. It was amazing to discover just how many there was and just how close we were a large community of like minded people.

The only time we went to a key swapping party was in the dead of winter and it had been some time since the incident at the man's house in the woods. We had been talking about it all that week and emailing each other, when we were supposed to be working. I had no idea what to expect and neither did he but we decided to make a day of it and go shopping in the city before heading out to the party.

I had booked to have my hair blow dried and have my nails done in the afternoon so we spent the morning shopping for sexy lingerie. I enjoyed trying on different outfits for my husband and we picked a nice one together. We settled on a zebra print bra and pants set with little pink bows and pink stitching. Later that day I had my nails painted pink to match and I bought new pink, open toed stilettos which also contained a pink flower on top.

I also purchased some hold-ups because I had laddered my tights and we were going straight to the party. It was a casual dress affair and my husband went in a new shirt he bought that day and the jeans he had on already.

I was wearing a black, high-waist pencil skirt along with a white blouse, unbuttoned to show off my bra (although you could clearly see the zebra print through it). I bought a pink, plastic, pearl necklace with large balls at the front which drew further attention to my cleavage and that was me. I never did the casual look outside of my house and to me, a skirt and shirt was dress down enough for a party.

When we arrived we were greeted at the door along with the other guests. The women were all given a badge with a number on it to wear. I was appalled at the thought of putting a large yellow badge onto my colour co-ordinated outfit so I held it in my hand. The men were ushered to a large cut-glass bowl in the hall which sat next to the telephone, on a pine sideboard and told to put their car keys inside before making their way to the living room.

It could have been anyone's sitting room, in anyone's house, in any suburban street. The walls were painted a cream and the sofas were nice dark brown leather. There were pictures on the mantelpiece of kids in school uniforms and crisps and dips were laid out for us on the coffee table.

My husband and I sat together, squeezed into a chair rather than joining others on the sofas. We were handed wine without being given the choice of red or white. I hated red wine then and still do so I just held it in my hand and smiled.

Looking around at the other couples I saw the usual wrinklies but interspersed between them were some middle-aged and even younger ones. One young man caught my eye and then my attention when he spoke. I didn't recognise his accent at first but I now know he was from South Africa. He had a mop of blonde hair and his wife too was blonde, although she looked older.

He appealed to me, more so than all the rest and I hoped I would end up with him. I wished we had been given a choice because I knew when he looked over, that he would've picked me.

Then the bowl came in carried by what I believed to be the organiser, a man in his late fifties with hair combed over from the side to hide his obvious baldness.

Inside the bowl where the men's keys but each had a large plastic tag attached which corresponded to the numbers on the women's badges. My husband was asked to pick first and his number coincided with a red-head sitting across from him. She rose when he called out the number and he followed her out of the room.

I became more and more nervous as the charade continued until there were only four of us left in the room and thankfully my blonde antipodean was still there, but he was last to pick.

Before him was a small dumpy man who was overweight and seemed to be sweating at just having to walk over to the bowl. He reached inside and I willed him to pick the other set. My heart pounded in my chest as I prayed he wouldn't pick my husbands keys. I knew the set and I watched his hand hover as it tried to choose. He reached it and touched the Audi sign on my husband's fob. I gulped but he then seemed to move it aside. That's it! I thought, he's going for the other but then as my shoulders tensed in excitement he changed his mind and lifted my husband's keys. He might have been trying to read the numbers but my badge was face down in the palm of my hand and I had held it tight so no-one could see.

He read out the number and I had no choice but to turn the badge to him. Then, however, as he walked toward me, he gallantly held out his hand to help me up from my seat. I carefully placed my untouched wine on the table before lifting my hand into his. It was clammy, sweaty and cold but he gripped me tight and led me away, away from the man I wanted to bed.

He led me back into the hall and then up the stairs. The badge and key numbers also corresponded to different rooms and thankfully ours was a bed room. My husband was not so lucky and ended up in a sitting room with his red-head. He did not enjoy his time with her and ended up having sex, sitting down, with her on his lap but with her back to him. There was no kissing and it had taken him ages to get an erection because he didn't fancy her and she had bitten fingernails, which was and still is, a major turn off for him. As a rule we didn't tell each other about our encounters but on that one occasion he told me afterward and we chuckled about his unfortunate evening.

I, on the other hand, had an altogether different experience. When we reached our allocated room we sat next to one another on the bed and he began by complimenting me on what I was wearing. He was saying all the right things as he lifted his hand and then took my necklace in his fingers. He asked me about it and I told him it was only £5.99 but he seemed pleased with the effort I had made to dress and accessorise. He continued complimenting me and talking about my body as his fingers let go of my necklace and began to unbutton my blouse. I was filled with pride at his words and I guess turned on by them. He began to tell me how he had prayed that he would pick me and had been anxious as each man before him chose their keys. I didn't want to tell him that I was praying for the opposite so I kept quiet and let him carry on.

He gently removed my blouse and then kissed me. His hand touched my face as we kissed and then my neck, then shoulder, until it slid all the way down my arm, taking my hand once again in his at the bottom.

We sat there for a short while like that as he held my hand and we kissed before I pulled back and said, 'Do you want me to take my bra off?' 'Oh no', he said shaking his head, 'I like it' and then his kissing became more passionate.

He was an amazing kisser, soft, gentle and very sensual and I could've kissed him like that for ages as he continued to stroke my arm, shoulders, neck and face. Eventually he stopped and asked me to remove my skirt but to leave my stockings and shoes on. He was such a gentleman and the way he asked I could do nothing but say yes. I did as he obliged and then I lay on the bed and watched as he de-robed.

I can only describe him as an ugly man with an ugly body. Nothing was as it should be. He had no hair on his head but an abundance of it between his legs. His penis was tiny, the smallest I had ever seen and his belly sat out in front of him, as if he was carrying a flesh coloured beach ball around with him. His arms were short and he had stubby, fat fingers. Above the beach-ball sat a pair of man boobs that would rival any you would see in a newspaper. His face too was round and he had no hair on his head apart from his eyebrows. He was nothing like the men I had been dreaming about all week as I sat in work waiting for the weekend.

We lay beside one another, him naked and me with my underwear on, including my hold-ups and shoes! It was, however, a very special time we shared together on that bed, as we kissed and stroked each others bodies. His kissing got even better and his compliments kept flowing making me feel nicer and more proud than ever before. I loved it, that time we were sharing and it made me want him. It made me see past his looks and flab and into his soul which was perfectly formed.

I took his tiny penis in my hand and his hands found their way inside my pants. He stopped kissing my lips as he moved his head down, kissing my neck then all the way down to my stomach. He kissed my pants and then removed them, carefully slipping them off past my shoes. He came back to me kissing my legs and feeling the stockings in his hands before returning to his position beside me. I left my bra on but removed my pearls as they were digging into my neck.

He told me he loved watching my hand with its pink fingernails feeling him and we lay there while I stoked him and he watched. I was filled with a serene peace as we lay there aside one another touching and feeling each others bodies. He then slowly moved his hand down until it was between my legs. I lay still as he fingered me and rubbed me, stopping occasionally to kiss me and to watch my hands on him. His fingers then found the top of my clitoris and rubbed hard sending pleasure throughout my soul. I couldn't hold back and I wanted him in me.

I tried pulling him onto me but he shoved his leg between mine sliding it up between my legs until it met his hand and shoved it harder into that spot on my clit. That was it; I had to have him there and then so I just said it, 'Fuck me'. His leg slid again banging his hand once more against me and he shoved his thumb inside. 'Fuck me, please!' He smiled and climbed on top before resting his penis on that very spot, teasing me as he held himself up with his arms.

I never wanted sex as much as I did right then. I looked into his eyes, 'Fuck me' I bit my bottom lip as I felt him throb against me. He reached down with his right hand taking his weight on his left and took hold of his tiny shaft. I was sure he was going to guide it in slowly but instead he slid his knob up and down, parting my lips which were now salivating with moisture. My back arched as his tip reached mine and once again he rubbed that spot! I pushed my pelvis up towards him, 'Please' I said, 'I want you inside me' but before I finished he was inside and my body fell back taking his heavy weight and feeling his tiny penis as it sent an electric shock through my body before he pulled out.

I was taken aback but I knew by his facial expression he would return. Sure enough another shock entered me, followed by yet another bolt then once again he was out. He was not blessed by size, or looks, nor was he fit but this man was a demon in bed, possessed by the sexiest, most romantic and somewhat dangerous devil of all. One who could direct a lightening bolt from the sky and into a woman's body then again, WOW, another bolt, this time sending shock waves in tiny ripples all over my skin. Then it settled as he writhed about inside and I lay there, hands above my head taking it all in.

Suddenly, out of the blue and whilst inside he started talking, 'I wanted you so bad'. 'You are amazing; I wanna touch you again, everywhere'. His words were like the opposite of his demonic side as if they came from heaven itself. I couldn't help but smile as my body joined his in a gentle rhythm and he lay beside me, touching me but still inside me. He felt the underside of my arms and it tickled, he felt my hands and it was sensual. He slid his fingertips all over my body and I loved it.

His heavenly touch was simply divine and he continued to deliver the compliments, in between sweet tender kisses, like an angel, as he said and did everything right.

'Can I see your nipples?' he eventually said and without a word in reply I pulled down my bra on one side to expose my breast to him. He leaned over and kissed my nipple. He didn't suck it but flicked his tongue back and forth across it and the wild passion that began our session slowly made its return.

He was still inside me when his fingers slid down past my belly button and settled once again on that spot. It drove me wild as he rubbed at it, bucked into me and flicked my nipple with his tongue.

He then kissed me and for the first time our kissing became snogging and then frantic licking as he rubbed me harder down below. Then in a flash the angel shot back to heaven and the demonic possession once again took hold. He pulled out and moved me onto my front and then slid in from behind.

He bucked into me from behind sending another bolt in, then another, followed by another, building up speed and power. I lifted my bum upwards towards him and to get his tiny penis in deeper and then without warning, SLAP!

His hand smacked my backside. Then again, SLAP! The bolts kept shooting into me with a force that pushed my face deep into the pillow. I was screaming in ecstasy as each bolt struck, my sound muffled by the pillow but the slaps sent my body intro convulsions and my mind racing. My screaming became louder and then more controlled until I began shouting, 'Oh Yeah', then a pause, then, 'Oh Yeah' then I continued, 'Oh yeah', 'Oh Yeah', 'Oh Yeah', 'Oh Yeah' and I couldn't stop.

I lifted my head to get air in and the sound out. My shouting became much louder and faster, 'Oh Yea, Oh Yea, Oh Yea, Oh Yea, OH YEA!' until I was consumed by a magnificent orgasm.

It was then as if his demon was transferred into my body and I turned on him throwing him down and jumping on top. I bounced up and down on him and pulled my bra down completely before grabbing his hands and holding them tight against my boobs. I squeezed his hands making him feel and grope me, holding his hands tightly in mine, until we came together and I collapsed in a heap beside him.

Perhaps that demon is still inside me? I don't know but I did learn one valuable lesson that night, never judge a book by its cover.

Chapter Nine — It Didn't Always Work Out

My husband and I didn't really like the swinging scene, despite my one great experience and as I said before there were usually too many wrinklies. We didn't like the fact that there was no choice of who you might end up going to bed with so we decided to have our own parties. We searched for like minded couples on the internet, sometimes going to their houses and sometimes with them coming to ours. It was good fun and when both of us got on with our new partners we would spend the night with them leaving after, or sometimes before breakfast the next day and never seeing them again.

It didn't always work out though as I remember one evening when we had a couple round for dinner and drinks to our house. We had been chatting with them on the internet and had seen pictures of them and they seemed nice. When they arrived, however, they were easily ten years older than the pictures and I couldn't warm to the guy at all. My husband seemed to be getting on ok with his wife so I didn't say anything.

I was wearing soft black leggings and a black satin top. I knew they were soft when I bought them and nice to touch and my husband confirmed this when he felt my bum before our guests arrived. The top was just long enough to cover my backside so I didn't need to wear a skirt and I had on a nice black bra which lifted my boobs. I had been out earlier and had got my nails French Polished for the evening and a blow dry at the hair dressers so I knew I was looking good but I just didn't feel good.

I wasn't feeling horny at all and as I sat on one side of the table with my guy my husband sat opposite and beside his lady for the evening. I longed to be beside my husband as his banter seemed more enjoyable. My guy was boring, not my type at all and I just wasn't feeling attracted to him. He kept grabbing my leg under the table. I don't know why he seemed to be hiding it but each time I sat down he would pat me on top of my thigh under the table. The softness of my leggings must have got to him because at one point he just kept his hand there making it difficult for him to eat. During the meal I could feel his hand on me, his fingers inching slowly under my leg until he began sliding his hand back and forth towards my knee but never too far away from it.

At one point he seemed to grab at my leg as if the tension was building inside him, grabbing my thigh tightly in his grasp. Every-time I got up he followed me in and out of the kitchen. Not content with my leg he kept also grabbing my ass and feeling me up from behind. At one point I could feel his hands sliding up and down the backs of my legs before he left to return to the table and sit down ahead of me. He became less shy about his groping as I served the coffee standing next to him. He slid his hand from the back of my knee up my leg grabbing and groping my ass in front of our partners. I smiled lightly towards my husband as his finger tips reached around almost touching my vagina.

When the meal was over I headed to our bar to get a another drink and as I left the room I saw my husband ,with his partner, on the sofa looking at each other, holding hands and playing with each others fingers. He seemed to be enjoying himself but before long my stalker was once again behind me. This time though, fuelled by the brandy he was drinking, he sank his hands inside my leggings at the back so he was holding my bare cheeks in his hands. I thought to myself, I'm going to have to put a stop to this, no way am I going to have sex with this man! but I also wasn't going to spoil the evening.

I yanked his hands out and led him by the hands into another smaller sitting room of ours at the front of the house. We hadn't used it in a while and it was a little cold. No light was on but the blinds were open and the room was lit only by the moonlight coming through the blinds.

I asked him to sit on the sofa and I sat next to him. I tugged at his trousers and asked him to remove them. I did the same to his boxers saying, 'These too'. As he removed them he slid back into the sofa almost lying down with his semi-erect penis pointing upwards and resting on his small pot belly.

I raised my hand and slowly moved it towards him

using my knuckles and the back of my hand I stroked his side and down to the top of his leg close to his penis but without touching it and then finally spreading out my fingers into the hairs on his leg.

I raised my hand again this time fingers dangling as I used my finger tips to lightly touch his penis starting at the top and working down as I saw it rise in the moonlight. It danced in the moonlight as if it was trying to reach up itself to touch my fingers. It bobbed wildly as if it had a mind of its own and I watched it as I stroked it gently then slid my finger-tips down its shaft. When my fingers reached the bottom I lay my hand down so that his knob was in the palm of my hand and I rested it there.

I then slid my hand down further, slowly tickling his balls with my finger tips until my hand cupped them and I gently massaged them. His penis was fully erect and still dancing on its own, lifting away from its owner and leaving a gap underneath. I slid my hand under the gap and it brushed the back of my hand. When my hand was underneath it I felt his hair in my fingers before flicking back my fingers and grabbing hold of his shaft. I grabbed at it hard like he had been grabbing at me and I yanked at it a couple of times almost hurting him as I pulled at it before lifting my hand away.

I went back again using my finger tips and lightly touching the tip as it bounced up and down with my touch, dancing once more in moonlight before I set my hand on top of it, as I had done previously and feeling once again his knob which was warmer and throbbed in my palm. I then slid down again and cupped his balls more firmly that time but not too hard.

He was frantically grabbing at my tits but as it was a push up bra it was hard to touch and not very exciting so I pulled down the straps of my top and then my bra straps to the elbow resting them in the crook of my arm. I then pulled my bra down to the underside of my breasts giving him full view and easy access to my fantastic chest.

He licked his lips when he first caught sight of my dark nipples and couldn't wait to grope me but I turned my attention once more to him.

I licked my hand and moistened my fingers with saliva and then placed my hand back onto his dancing dick, sliding my thumb underneath so I could pull at him. I stroked him up and down, bottom to top, faster and faster, slowing sometimes to rub his knob and tease him while he groped wildly at my tits.

I kept licking my fingers and rubbing my spit onto his knob which seemed to drive him crazy each time my warm touch returned.

Eventually I jerked and jerked in a gentle rhythm until he came. I never saw spurts like that before, one then two then three. I pulled my hand away before the remainder of his spunk spilled out and I covered myself again before handing him the tissues we keep beside the sofa.

I told him I would leave him there to relax and as I left he was still in the same position slumped into the sofa.

I then went looking for my husband still not turned on at all by the grabbing at my tits.

I saw my husband through the slightly open living room door. He was on his knees on the floor, naked from the waist down and banging at the lady while she was doubled over onto the sofa. He was taking her from behind and her face was buried in the cushion to muffle her moans. Maybe he didn't fancy the look of her either, I thought but as I looked I couldn't stop staring. I was watching my husband's face and his hands as they held her bare ass. I got so turned on I started feeling myself, rubbing between my legs and through the soft leggings. They were soft, lovely to touch in fact and I thought to myself, no wonder he couldn't keep his hands away from them earlier.

They left soon after that and I took my hubby upstairs. We had fantastic sex that night and I will always remember that night, watching my husband having sex and the expression on his face as he entered that lady.

Chapter Ten - The Young Guy

I was beginning to get annoyed at trying to swing with other couples and was a lot more comfortable when we just organised our own house party. A healthy mix of swingers and non-swingers were invited and mixed with sound, single people who were up for a laugh. Friends of friends turned up and sometimes people we saw again and again came, along with others we saw only once or twice.

At one of those parties, at our house, a young guy followed me everywhere. He was a lot younger than me but cute and in our garden, at that time, we had a big wooden shed with a pool table in it and that night he kept asking me to go out with him for a game. I wouldn't normally have minded but it was the middle of winter and that night it was freezing. I was wearing this tiny black dress, which showed off both legs and cleavage and obviously caught the attention of this young guy because he followed me all around the place and seemed obsessed with holding my hand when we were chatting to people. Even when my husband was there he was touching me but it always out of sight, almost sneakily (which I didn't like at first) but then his attentions began to turn me on. He would feel my bum and run his hand up and down my back as I was chatting away to my friends and the more I had to drink the more I liked it.

Finally his begging paid off and I agreed to go out to the shed with him but as it was dark outside we had to take it slowly over the paving stones. I was in high heels and had to hold on to him to keep steady. I guess his immaturity got the better of him and he couldn't wait until we reached the shed. He took my arm and spun me round to face him and then pushed me backwards. He pressed me up against the wall of the house and started kissing me. I was carrying a drink so it was awkward but by that time I was tipsy and he was a great kisser so I let him carry on. His hands began sliding up my dress onto my bum and then quickly inside my pants. It was a bit too much and I didn't realise what was going on until I realised he had his cock out and was trying to pull aside my pants to shag me up against the wall.

It was all a bit rushed so I stopped him and thankfully he calmed down. 'I thought we were going to play pool' I slurred as he kindly put his cock away. He seemed to take it the wrong way and appeared to be in a huff when we began to play pool but before long he became aroused again as he watched me taking shots and my dress slid up, exposing my knickers to him, as I stretched to pot the pool balls. He took every opportunity to grope me and fondle me as I walked around the table playing a game he had no interest in.

I wanted him to kiss me again. I really enjoyed his earlier kiss but he seemed intent only on feeling me up. He hadn't yet touched my breasts and I thought

I would use my secret weapons to keep him busy so I could slow things down to my pace but before I could reveal them my husband and another guy arrived to play pool themselves.

As our game finished we played a game of doubles. I could see this poor young guy feeling rejected, feeling like he'd missed his moment but to keep him going every time he hit a good shot I would kiss him on the lips, in celebration. He obviously didn't know that my husband wouldn't mind and that's why, I thought, he had been sneaky all night but then I thought, perhaps that was his way. I didn't know for sure, In fact I knew nothing about him and after that night I never saw him again.

As the game was coming to an end I would sit on his knee between shots and again his hands would wonder. Yet again he would be trying to hide them, sneakily hiding his actions and attempting to cover up his intentions. At one point he slid his hand inside my dress and very nearly got to the prize but I had to get up for another shot.

My hubby could see clearly what was happening. He wasn't stupid and was ready to leave us alone after the game but this guy didn't know and I could feel his pain as he patiently waited on more time alone with me. Before my husband left though I gave him an amazing snog, with my hand on his crotch and I noticed he was hard at the thought of this young guy and me.

Eventually the guy got what he came for.

As soon as we were alone he came over to me, probably thinking he had little time before someone else would come for a game but I knew my husband wouldn't have let anyone come out so I was relaxed. Luckily the heaters were on because it was very cold outside and I wanted to see all of this guy. He was beautiful all over and I wasn't having a quick fumble with clothes on as I wanted to see and feel his body. He approached me again with his hands out-stretched before him. 'Slow down', I said, 'no-one will be back out here. Just kiss me.' As he kissed me I undid the buttons on his jeans and dropped them to the floor whilst his hands were up my back and groping my bum, grabbing at it. My hands wandered inside his boxers and took hold of his pulsating penis. I had never felt one as hard and clearly ready. The guy was dying for me and I was well aware of how badly he wanted me.

Before I knew it his hands were inside my pants again, yanking at them to get them off and it wasn't long before I realised the guy wasn't interested in my breasts. I thought to myself, he just wants to fuck me and I opened his shirt and kissed his chest but he was working fast. My pants were off in a flash and then his thumb and fingers were inside me. My head was spinning with the wine and his pace and I could hardly catch my breath between the thrusts with his hand. I knew then there was going to be no oral sex just straight down to business. I knew this guy was going to come and he wanted to get inside before it was too late.

I was a little taken aback by the speed and in the haste forgot about a condom. I had him nearly naked at that point but most of what happened next is a blur. I couldn't take my eyes off his beautiful body and then for a brief moment I was the one with uncontrollable hands all over him. I was sliding my hands all over his muscles and torso when he then lifted me onto the pool table. I wanted him to take me slower and to fuck me from behind. I had imagined it when I was playing pool and leaning over the table. I wanted to stop him but his kissing was great, really intense and then it came… wham! He was inside me before I knew, thrusting forward and banging hard into me.

It was fantastic sex but I never understood why he didn't take it slower, savour the moment, feel my breasts even. I had fantastic boobs which he could have enjoyed for ages but he just kissed me then fucked me and when he was finished he was busy dressing before I had even caught my breath.

I did kiss him again before he left that night. A long lingering snog but that was it; one rushed drunken encounter and one passionate embrace and then he was never to be seen again.

Chapter Eleven - Two Guys, One Night

I remember one Sunday when I was lazing about the house wearing a white vest top and jeans, no bra on and no socks or shoes. My husband had invited a few friends around to watch the footie so I decided to read a book I had bought for the occasion. You know the type, erotic but romantic novel. I was lazing on a big old sofa we have at the bottom of the kitchen resting my head against its arm, legs outstretched in front of me on the sofa book in my hands at my waist as I began reading. The window to the back garden was at the other end of the sofa and I could see it was a lovely day outside.

Occasionally the sunlight peeked out from behind a cloud finding it's was through the window and onto my bare feet, warming them as if it was my own personal ray of sunlight. My back was to the kitchen door, which was opened and led along the hall to the front door so I heard his mates arriving but I didn't turn around to say hello as I was engrossed in my book. I'm sure they saw me reading as the veered off the hall and into the living room but no-one acknowledged me.

I could hear the chatter and the noise from the TV but it didn't distract me from my novel. Occasionally someone would come in to collect beers from the fridge and I knew some of his friends but not all. The ones I knew asked how I was to which I replied fine not wanting to start up a conversation. Then a different approach as one of his friends came up behind me looking over my shoulder and asked me what I was reading. I didn't want to be rude so I began telling him the story about the two lovers. I then felt something. At first I didn't know what it was, because it was so light, until he pressed the weight of his hands fully onto my shoulders. I didn't move as I continued with the story, feeling the warmth of his hands sinking into my shoulders with the sunlight on my feet I felt heat at each end of my body. His hands seemed to tremble as I told of how the lovers spent the night together. His thumbs began massaging my neck gently as I disclosed their sexual encounter and then his left hand became lighter. I could no longer feel its warmth but I could feel it shaking as it moved, edging forward. His fingertips lightly caressed the front of my neck and then further down my chest before one swift movement took his hand straight inside my vest. I wasn't expecting it but my body remained motionless as his left hand was now holding my left breast. My story telling was getting more erratic and my breathing heavier as my concentration shifted from what I was saying to what I was feeling. His warm hand was holding my breast and my nipple was rising into the palm of his hand as the heat from his hand surged into my body through my breast, warming me all over as he gently massaged my boob.

A shout came, 'Hurry up with them beers!' and he was

gone. His hand was gone and the warmth had gone along with it. I felt like all my heat had left with his hand as he whisked it away in a flash and I shivered as I regained my composure. I sat quivering before realising I had no idea who he was or what he looked like. I felt different, kinda strange, I wasn't sure at first what I felt until I realised I wanted more. I questioned myself, why did he do this? Would he do it again? Oh how I willed it. I wanted it. I wanted his hand on me again, feeling me and making me warm.

I tried to read on but couldn't concentrate, waiting on each beer run and hoping it would be my guy but he never returned. Different men came and went with their beer but not my guy.

I eventually got up and decided to make a start on dinner. I remember standing in the kitchen chopping carrots when he finally arrived. We glanced at one another and he looked away, sheepishly, as he took the beers from the fridge and set them on the breakfast bar.

I willed him to come to me, in my mind longing for him and then he answered my call. He came up beside me and asked me what I was making. I hadn't seen him before and didn't know for sure it was him at first until I saw his sheepish look and then I certain. It was further confirmed when he spoke as I remembered his voice. Seeing him for the first time made me want him even more. He had beautiful blue eyes and lovely lips that I wanted to touch. When I answered him by simply saying, 'I'm making stew', I lifted a piece of chopped carrot up to his mouth. I was dying to touch his beautiful lips and as he took the carrot in his mouth his lips kissed my fingers. They were soft and moist and I loved the way they gently stroked my finger tip and as I drew my hand away he came behind me, leaning over my shoulder as I continued to chop. Then he whispered in my ear, 'Tell me more about your book, about the lovers?' His warm breath sent shivers down my spine and my body tingled in anticipation of his touch.

I closed my eyes and began to tell him once again about what I had read before feeling his hands on my hips. I could feel his thumbs going to work and caressing my back before his fingers fumbled their way inside my vest top. I almost licked my lips when his warm fingers found my skin tingling my sides with excitement. That time his right hand quivered, as I retold the story, before inching upwards towards the underside of my breast. I had the knife gripped tightly in my right hand, knuckles white and clenched around it, as my body tightened in anticipation of his warm gentle touch. I felt my left hand leave the counter and fall to my side as if it had a mind of its own. All my concentration was fixed on his right hand under my right breast. Please feel me, I was thinking as my left arm swung under his and around my back finding his crotch and resting there. I then gripped his hard shaft tightly through his jeans and he finally slipped his hand up to my breast, cupping it firmly before massaging gently, just as he had done before.

It felt like heaven as my body eased and I let go of the knife. My other hand slid firmly up and down the front of his jeans and I could feel his body arch towards me but then it was over in a flash, just like before. No-one called him that time but he still felt that his time was up and so he let go and turned away. Grabbing the beers as he walked past he didn't even turn to look at me.

He left me wanting more, wanting to feel his lips again and to feel his warmth as we kissed. I wanted to kiss him so badly!

I stayed in the kitchen willing his return but he didn't come back and when the footie was over everyone left.

I wondered about him for a while after that and about the little things like his name, where he was from and how he knew my husband. I chatted to my husband to find out details, anything at all but I never really found out much. I didn't want to ask too many questions for fear I would alert my husband to my desire for his friend.

I was therefore surprised, but very excited, when he turned up at one of our parties. It was a swinging party but although there were about 4 couples there swapping partners I had invited some girl-friends to make it more of a party and he had invited some of his mates to make up the numbers. I was happy to see him but disappointed also as I was already matched that night with another man. His wife was spending the evening with my husband.

He was a nice man, older than me and quite distinguished. He had a good job and was smartly dressed in a suit and open necked shirt. He had a thick head of dark hair with some grey through it. He had swarthy skin and small dark eyes with a big wide grin.

He was pleasant and I enjoyed his company but he didn't exactly set my world alight. I got chatting to him and we sat together on the sofa.

My mind was wondering though to my other guy, my husband's footie friend, my handsome stranger, my groper even. I caught his eye a few times and it sent shivers down my spine, like the shivers when he left me the first time. It was as if my body shivered without him, needing him.

I sat with my date for the evening on the sofa facing him. He was at one end of the sofa turned to me and I was in the middle turned to him. One of my legs was lifted onto the sofa and my foot was resting under the other leg which was rooted to the ground. He too was turned to me in a similar way. I was wearing a short black cotton dress. From the front it looked like a baggy sweatshirt but it was backless, tied behind the neck with a fine cord. It covered my backside, just about as if it was a short skirt all the way round. Without a back I couldn't wear a bra but my boobs were fully covered at the front.

My right arm rested on the back of the sofa, as did his left so our hands were touching where they met. We were feeling each others hands as we chatted, sliding our fingers up and down each others, my nails sometimes tickling the palm of his hand. It felt nice. As we stared into each other's eyes his other hand gently stroked my leg in front of him. His finger tips tickled it at times. My other hand would occasionally find the top of his leg also and I would rub his leg using my nails to gently scratch it as I pulled my hand back toward me.

I was thinking about our hands when I felt something touch my back. I could no longer concentrate on my hands as they began to fix their position, no longer moving.

It was like a knuckle sliding up my spine from the base of my back up to my neck and down with more knuckles joining it as it sank towards my bum. Then finger tips sliding up my back and down again teasing my skin and making me tingle all over. A firm palm of a hand then took control feeling my back, not just up and down my spine but all over in a circular motion. It was warm and soft and I thought it might be my guy so I said nothing.

The hand became adventurous and went to my right side next to the sofa. My back was warm and my side getting hotter as it reached around and grabbed at my boob. I knew it was my guy as I had I felt his gentle groping before and recognised the warmth of his hand as once again my nipple rose to greet him. The man in front of me had no idea what was going on or how horny I was feeling but just in case he found me out, I took my left hand and lifted it to his face. I'm sure I breathed in air as my nipple was pinched.

I took his face in my hand and pulled him to me kissing him and snogging him wildly as my guy groped my breast.

Then just as he had done each time before he was gone, slipping away without a word and without me noticing as my tongue was tied to my man for that night. I wanted to be with the guy not with that man I wanted things to be different. I was looking around for him after that every time I went for a top up or to the toilet until I eventually found him in the kitchen chatting to a girl. She had her arms locked around his waist as they laughed and chatted. I wanted to be that girl, to be close to him, to have his warm gentle hands on me again. I was actually jealous! I couldn't believe it at first but I was green with envy as I watched them and chatted to my friend. I waited until she finally let go of him, perhaps to get another drink, but she left him alone and I saw my chance. I raised my head towards him nodding at him and then gestured with my head for him to follow me. As I left the kitchen he followed me into the utility room and I headed to the back-door where he caught up with me. 'Come with me' I said. It was cold outside, too cold for what I was wearing but I didn't care I wanted him to know I wanted him. I wanted his lips again and his hands. I pulled him into the shadows and asked him to kiss me.

As we kissed his hands were gliding up and down my bare back and I loved how he caressed every inch warming it again as before. Our lips felt perfect together as his gentle kisses became stronger, our mouths worked in tandem as we snogged each other. Great snog! I thought to myself, I like this guy a lot!

His hands slipped down over the skirt part at the bottom of my dress onto my bum and then under cupping my cheeks and gently massaging them, as he had done to my breasts, sending warm waves of excitement rushing up my body from my ass.

I eventually stopped and pulled away saying, 'I have to

go… its freezing out here'. Once again as his hands left my body it shivered with cold. My teeth were chattering as his hands had gone and yet again they had seemed to drain the heat from my body.

He begged me to stay with him, to spend the night with him or just to go to bed with him but I couldn't. I had my date for the evening and I had already left him alone for too long.

'I'll give you a quick blow job', I said as I unbuttoned his jeans and pulled out his cock. It too was warm as I held it in my cool hands before kneeling in front of him. I placed it into my mouth and sucked hard. I was too cold and I couldn't stay there much longer so I stood up leaving him unfinished said sorry and left. I left him there hanging out, hanging out outside in the shadows.

I had to get back inside, back to the heat and comfort of the house and back to my man, my date for the evening.

Sure enough there he was still on the sofa looking forlorn. I felt sorry for him as I made my excuses saying that I had got chatting but his face kept its upset expression. He only smiled when I asked him to come upstairs.

When we reached the bedroom the party was dying down but I could still hear the dull thud of music coming from below.

It was late but not too late maybe one o'clock in the morning but he seemed tired as we walked up the stairs.

He was a kind man and very gentle he just didn't light my fire. He stood behind me in the bedroom, next to the bed, staring at my reflection in the mirror in front of me as he gently undid the strap at my neck allowing the front of my dress to fall and show him, in the reflection, a taste of what was to come. He then pulled the rest of my dress down lowering himself to his hunkers as he helped it off my feet. I was standing there now in my high heels and pants as he slid his hands up the back of my legs past my ass up my back and onto my shoulders. He held my shoulders and kissed then before kissing at my neck. My head fell back as he kissed my neck and licked my ear. He whispered in my ear, 'Lie down on the bed'. I turned and lay on the bed as he had asked. Sitting beside me he began to feel my legs, like he had done before on the sofa but firmer, sliding the palms of his hands up and down my legs then over my pants and up my belly before groping my breasts and then back down again. On the way down he kindly removed my pants and began caressing my inner thighs. His hands were sliding closer and closer to where he wanted them to be. He started to kiss my legs and then my inner thighs and then my moist lips as he parted my clitoris with his fingers. His tongue quickly licked my clitoris, lashing in and out. My body was aching as it arched upwards, aching not for this man but for my guy.

I lay and dreamt about my guy. I began to recall the memory of our first encounter, the feeling of him behind me, his shaky hands, then his hand feeling me up and then again in the kitchen later that day.

My memory was drawn to earlier that night, to his

kiss and to his tender lips as the man ate at my pussy. Waves of intense pleasure flowed through my body from between my legs invading my soul as I orgasmed, still thinking about my guy. Lying there, head deep in the pillow, I didn't even realise that the man's tongue had gone and that his penis was creeping in, until it was fully inside.

It was large and took my breath away for a second as he banged it in, thrusting forward and sinking me deeper into the pillow. His body fell onto me, His weight felt like it was crushing my lungs as he lay on me. His hands were underneath me, under my bum, pulling it towards him. He was pushing his cock further and deeper inside, hurting me, until I felt his body tighten and then relax allowing me to catch a breath before he rolled off.

I lay there for ages. I had enjoyed the orgasm but still wanted more. I was still horny at the though of my guy, my groper.

I played with myself as I lay there feeling my boob trying to imagine it was him but it was no good. I felt unsatisfied by this man who was by then sleeping next to me.

I got up and decided to go downstairs. I don't know why but I went down naked. I was feeling really randy and didn't know what I would encounter, maybe a couple having sex? Maybe I could join them? I wondered as I crept down the stairs.

The party was over and the music off. Bottles of beer

and wine glasses littered the living room, some on the floor, others strewn about the place resting anywhere and everywhere. Some looked full some half full but most empty.

We had two sofas in the living room and each contained a body. The farthest from me had a man with his back to me and he was curled up and seemed to be asleep with a jacket of some description covering him for warmth, like a blanket.

The other sofa contained a drunken bloke who appeared to be awake and mumbling to himself, eyes half open and half shut.

I looked down at him as I stood over him and lifted his hand. I slid it up between my legs letting him feel my inner thigh until his thumb reached my very wet pussy but I got no reaction and as I let go the hand and arm dropped to the floor.

I thought about sitting on this guy and riding him but there was no mission of him getting erect so I walked away into the kitchen.

I opened the fridge looking for a drink. It was filled with alcohol of different types and colours. Blue WKD, cider, beer, wine but then I saw a carton of orange juice, opened the lid and took a big gulp to wet my mouth.

As I closed the fridge I was startled by something, someone and as my eyes adjusted again after the brightness of the fridge light I realised it was my guy. I asked him if that was him on the other sofa to which he replied, 'Yes I couldn't sleep.' I couldn't stop thinking about you.' 'Me neither' I said before I realised I was naked. His eyes were all over me looking at me up and down and wanting me with a desire I had not yet seen from him.

I held out my hands and took his hands in mine then walked backwards until the kitchen counter stopped me from going any further. I then slid my body up to sit on the counter as he drew closer to me. My legs parted as if to say come in and he brought his body inside.

He leant in to kiss me and again I enjoyed one of the best kisses ever as he snogged me.

Again his hands slid up and down my back as my hands once more unbuttoned his jeans to drop them to the floor. My hands quickly found his cock again and I couldn't help but pull it towards me, willing it inside. His hands found my breasts and yet again they were warm and gentle as he massaged them. He was inside me in a second and it was fantastic, far better than the man upstairs. He didn't hurt me with his thrusts and as we grinded together he enjoyed my breasts even more and nibbled on my nipples, sucking and licking at them.

He took one of my breasts in his hand and held it like he was squeezing a bottle of water into his mouth. My nipple formed the nozzle of the bottle as it rose with his sucking. He squeezed as if to release the water into him and my nipple quivered inside his mouth as he drew in hard. He then lashed his tongue back and forth across it still holding and gently squeezing my breast.

The flickering was warm and lush and as I watched his mouth take me inside I held his head against my breast, holding him to the bosom that first drew him to me and us together.

My hands then slid down past his neck and onto his back and my nipple throbbed and then shivered when he stopped sucking as once again my warmth left along with him. He stood straight upright as he rose again to kiss me and my hands went up his back, under his t-shirt, scratching his skin with my nails. His kiss was even better than before and I found my nails digging into him and scratching his back as his tongue met mine. With each long scratch he moaned and fucked me harder; bang, bang, bang, banging inside me as I jumped up and down on the kitchen counter. Jumping and bouncing wildly as he banged and banged and then wrapping my legs around him pulling him tighter to me, pulling him deeper inside me until we came together.

I glanced over his shoulder and saw the guy from the sofa. He was there, at the fridge, just standing staring at us but I ignored him and turned again to my guy for another wonderful snog as his hardness died inside me. It slipped out eventually and he just turned and left, just as before without a word. Suddenly and swiftly he turned and disappeared leaving me dripping on the counter but satisfied.

I went back upstairs after that looking for my husband. He was in the guest bedroom sleeping in bed with his lady for the evening, my man's wife. They were both sleeping but not together and with their backs to one another so I got into bed in front of my husband, pulled his arm over me and went to sleep.

Chapter Twelve – The Elderly Man

My husband and I were invited to someone's party. It wasn't a swinging party, as such, so we decided to give it a go. It was a swinger who owned the house so we knew what it would be might be like but we hadn't been out for ages, having had most of our own parties at home and so we decided to accept. When we arrived though we wished once again we had stuck to our rule and left well alone, especially as there were a lot of older people there. Wrinklies everywhere!

My husband and I had drunk a bottle of wine between us before we left home but as he wanted to be well on his way to being drunk by the time we arrived, I was almost sober and wanted to keep my wits about me.

It was a grand old house, massive in fact, out in the country with lots of luxurious cars parked outside in a courtyard decorated by stone paving and potted plants.

We walked inside the main room which was really an extension of the hall-way and which opened up into an enormous reception room almost oval in shape, lined by wood panelled on the walls and tiled floors underfoot.

The room was lit by ornate chandeliers which seemed to be dripping with diamonds as they sparkled above us. It was the grandest house I had ever been in and certainly the biggest.

A gathering of champagne glasses sat on the side on a table draped in a pure white tablecloth and we took one each as we passed. I was wearing my purple dress, long and figure hugging so no pants could be worn for fear they would show. It was also very low cut at the both the front and back as it plunged deep from the shoulders and so therefore no bra could be worn either. My breasts, my secret weapon, were perfectly formed so I was therefore able, at that time, to get away with a dress like that. It was my favourite dress back then and showed off my curves in a way that made me feel sexy and confident. I wore a new pair of Kurt Geiger pewter Mary Jane heels I had purchased to go with my dress. My husband was earning good money then and so was I so I began splashing out more on designer clothes and accessories but my favourite dress was a bargain I picked up from a dress hire shop. I wondered some times who might have hired it or worn it before but I was sure that no-one ever wore it like I did.

Naturally I turned a few heads as we walked through the crowd holding hands and immediately I noticed one elderly gentleman's eyes following me everywhere I went. As we mingled some couples we met wanted to swap partners for the evening but we turned them down! Eventually the elderly man who had been eyeing me up came over to us. I guessed he was in his sixties but still had his hair which was silver, very thick and parted at the side. I could tell he was once very attractive and was still handsome but old compared to us. We felt like teenagers compared to the others we saw there.

When he arrived he put out his hand for my husband to shake breaking our bond as we had been holding hands and I had been clutching him tight. I thought he might take my hand too but ignoring me at first he starting talking to my husband about wife swapping. Feeling my distress my hubby was quick to say that we would not be doing that tonight. I don't think he fancied going down on a wrinkly either! The man persisted though until he finally asked my husband could he feel my breast.

My dress was that kind that draws attention to the breast as you could see the whole sides of them and I watched many men imagine touching them as they stared at me when I wore it but before I could say anything my husband had nodded and his hand was inside cupping my breast. It wasn't that unusual as there were many sights around us of people fondling and kissing but it was unusual the way he just cupped it, no groping or looking for the nipple just resting it in his hand. His hand was warm and I was amazed as he kept his hand there and chatted to my husband about the weather while cupping my breast.

It was my left breast and he seemed disinterested in the right, perhaps it was the way he was standing or that it was his right hand but he eventually slid out and left. He left me intrigued but not excited, not wanting more but strangely sexy as if my body had lured him to me. As we continued mingling he was still watching me although I was no longer uneasy at his persistent glances.

He came back again but with a friend the second time and again ignoring me began chatting once more to my husband. All three were taking about breasts and again without asking me or even my husband that time he told his friend to feel me up. Before I knew it he had both his hands on me although it was over my dress, not inside and more of a quick grope than a feel.

My husband was lashing the champagne by this stage so when the other man asked him if he wanted to feel some nice breasts he was off like a shot to a group of ladies hands groping happily.

I was left with the elderly man, the man who seemed fascinated by my left breast and he finally introduced himself as the owner of the house taking my hand and kissing it but not letting go. We chatted until he realised I was not for staying much longer then he said, 'Why don't you and your husband go to my room?' He was suggesting we slope upstairs to be with each other but before I could make excuses he was pulling my hand taking me towards the stairs. Luckily I caught my husband's eye and he followed.

As we walked up the stairs, which seemed to never end, I had the man taking me in one hand while I pulled my husband along with the other. We walked along a long corridor until he opened a door into a fantastic room. It was like a hotel penthouse suite with a massive bed and a massive telly in front of it. My husband was feeling rather randy and was quite happy to oblige but as we entered the room the elderly man felt my bum, not like a young man would grabbing and groping at it but in a careful gentile & nice way. I didn't mind, after all we were getting the use of his room.

There were drinks on the side and my husband and I had our fair share. By that stage my hubby was steaming drunk but we managed to make love in our usual way. It was nice, familiar and afterwards we turned the TV on. I wasn't sure if the man was listening at the door but I was sure I had locked it.

Anyway, as usual, it wasn't long before my husband was asleep and The Matrix film was on screaming its imagery across the large screen. I was a bit light headed myself after drinking half the man's Gin so I decided to rest and leave after the film.

It wasn't long until I heard the door. I was sure I locked it but somehow in came the man, the elderly man, the breast man, the man whose room it was and there we were lying naked in his bed.

I nudged my husband under the covers but he was spark out.

The man approached the bed and I soon realised he too was completely naked. He wasn't bad for his age and his skin was tanned with a little grey hair on his chest and a little pot belly. His penis was hanging long and loose below him as he walked over and sat on the bed. I was nervous at first but soon at ease as he looked at me in the same way that he did when he had cupped my breast earlier.

I sat up in the bed like in the movies holding the sheet across my chest and trying to disguise the fact that I was naked. 'Can I see them?' he asked politely but before I could answer he gently pulled the sheet down revealing my breasts. At first he was fixated on the left and lifted his hand over towards it. He held it gently again with the palm of his hand on my nipple. I could feel his skin was quite hard this time as he massaged my left breast.

His left hand then touched my right breast but he used the back of his hand first sliding it up from under to over and across the nipple. I watched his left hand, following its movements as his right just held my breast firmly but gently in its grip.

Then he started to feel my right gently with his left hand. I felt weird, strange but calm as I sat upright in this man's bed watching as he played with my boobs. I felt like I had to do something and as I watched his penis raise to a semi-hard on, but no further, I was thinking to myself, maybe he cant get a hard on? I don't know why but I put my hand onto his penis. On top at first just touching it to see if it would rise. I could feel it stirring but much slower than I had been used to. I slid my fingers underneath and lifted it pulling my hands up and down it and making it harder and harder. As I continued his feeling became groping and his penis soon began to pulsate. This is mad! I thought, what if my husband wakes up? What if this man wants more?' I was getting turned on as I continued pleasuring him. I felt nice although I was worried he was going to try to kiss me but I didn't stop. I gave the best hand job of my life, slowly at first then long hard strokes until he came in my fingers still clutching my breasts.

His face was red by the time he came and his breathing heavy but he just sort of mimed with his lips the words, 'Thank-you' then got up and left.

I was sitting there stunned, too stunned to move and so I waited just in case he came back before I began to get dressed. I pulled my dress on, dragged my husband up to get dressed and we left.

I never told my husband about the elderly man but we decided after that night that we would no longer accept any invitations to swinger's parties and even discussed finishing with the whole swinging idea. For me though it was already too late as something inside me had already changed.

As each incident occurred I was becoming more and more adventurous. I was beginning to feel an urge inside me to be naughty and to do things behind my husband's back. I didn't like the thoughts I had at first but ever since that night when I had sex with his friend I felt different. It was the first time I had done something that he hadn't agreed to before hand and it felt different, better almost. The pre-arranged sex that night was flat and nothing like the sex I enjoyed on the kitchen counter while my husband was upstairs, asleep and unaware.

I was losing interest in swinging parties and swapping partners and I just wanted sex with strangers. I didn't care who or where or when but I began to fantasize about being groped in public and having sex in strange places with strange men and always without my husband's knowledge.

I resisted the urge to be bad at first that is until I met my husband's boss.

Chapter Thirteen – My Husband's Boss

I could tell my husband's boss liked me the first time we met. It was at a dinner party in our house and he was there alone (not with his wife). He'd heard about our wild parties and there were four other guys there from my husband's work and a girlfriend of mine just to try and even up the odds a bit.

My husband was doing all the cooking so I was at the dinner table all evening drinking wine, far too much wine (if truth be told) because I was getting very, very drunk. As the courses went on the eye contact with his boss got stronger but that's all it was at first. I was getting horny as I do when I drink wine but as it was work people I wanted to try and behave (as best I could anyway).

At one point after dinner when the party got going I was in the kitchen making tequila slammers when his boss came in. He came right up behind me, ever so close and I could feel the strength of him almost pushing into my back as he asked me what I was doing. I told him and asked him if he wanted one. I then felt his hands gently touching my hips as he said yes and I knew then that he wanted me.

I could tell by his eyes as well as his body language. I sucked my finger and dipped it into the salt bowl before lifting it to his mouth. As he opened I let him lick the salt from my finger before he took his shot. I was turned sideways to him now and his hand was resting on my bum (not below it or grabbing it just gently touching it). I handed him the slammer to down. I watched as his face winced with the taste before taking the lime and putting it into my mouth holding it between my teeth. I pushed my head to his so he could suck the lime gently touching my lips as he pulled the juice through his teeth.

I don't know why but then as I grabbed the tray of drinks in one hand my other hand gently stroked his crotch as I glided around the back of him and slipped into the living room. I must have been giving him a sign but I remember thinking, at the time, that I shouldn't have done that. After all it was my husband's boss and he was married! Maybe he didn't even swing?

After dinner and in the living room he sat next to me all night. The party got going and I spent most of it dancing with my girlfriend. Each time I sat down to rest it was always next to him, very close as there was little room left on the sofa between him and the end of it. I could swear the space got smaller every time I sat down. When most of the men were in the kitchen chatting he stayed in the living room watching me dance and hoping not to loose his spot on the sofa.

Near the end of the evening (for me anyway as I was too pissed to stay up much longer) my girlfriend had left to get drinks or go to the toilet or something and

I pulled his boss up to dance. He was reluctant to get on his feet but I dragged him up anyway. I started the dance looking at him and although a lot of that part of the evening is a blur I remember vividly turning and dancing with my back to him and grinding my hips so that my bum was rubbing against him. I remember he was hard and embarrassingly I remember reaching my hands around and stroking him as we danced.

I don't remember him touching me anywhere but my hips but I also remember putting my arms up and around his neck and pulling his head down to my neck. No kissing went on or anything else apart from the grinding and stroking.

I don't remember anything else about the party that night and must have gone to bed shortly after that dance. I don't know how long I was in bed for but I was lying fully clothed on top of the covers. I was wearing a short black dress, no bra as usual, with black lace panties and hold ups but I had, at least, kicked my shoes off before collapsing.

The next thing I remember is a feeling as I lay on my side. I could feel something at my back or lower. I was half asleep but half awake and had no energy to move any part of my body. It felt like it would take all my energy just to open my eyelids. The feeling was weird but I finally realised it was around the top of my legs and looking back now I know it was my pants being pulled down, not all the way but just to my knees. I then felt something pushing in and out between the top of my legs. I didn't know at the time what it was, a hand, a finger or even a penis? It wasn't going inside me just rubbing the lips of my vagina back and forth. I was wakening more but still too wrecked to move as it went on for a bit before I felt myself being turned and pulled back so I was no longer on my side but also not fully on my back. My knees were still bent and my arm was being pulled until my hand was touching something, holding something. I still couldn't open my eyes and my arm dropped beside me as my foot was pulled stretching my leg out and then opening my legs. I didn't know my dress had been pulled down exposing my breasts but I know they weren't touched. I felt something then inside me, hard then harder, banging in. It was kinda sticky down below and a little sore when the banging started but again I couldn't move and remember just lying there motionless. It was all over quickly but I remember when the banging was ending and as the thrusts shifted my body, rocking me back and forth, my eyes opened briefly with the force of the final thrust. It would have been accidentally as I didn't manage it myself and caused only by the force of being banged between my legs. As they opened though, I caught a glimpse of my husband's boss.

I didn't remember anything the next day but over time I have remembered bits and pieces and put the rest together in my mind. When I woke my breasts were exposed and my pants were hanging off one ankle. His boss must have left that night.

I didn't see him again for a while but my husband always commented on how his boss talked about me all the time.

I saw him again at another dinner party but he was

there with his wife and she knew he kept staring at me and was getting angry about it. The only words we exchanged were when he passed me in the hall at one point and said 'No slammers tonight?' and I replied, 'No not tonight' rather sheepishly. They left early that night with his wife in an obvious huff.

He kept pestering my husband at work to have another party and was aware of what our parties could be like so we invited him round again but that time it was only him and my husband and I invited two girls along just to see if he would go for them. Again all night, though, he was fixed on me.

My husband was delighted by the attention of the girls and at one point they were choosing CDs together and when I looked over there was a tangled web of legs over his. I couldn't tell who's were who's. Meanwhile I was at the table chatting to his boss who was really quite interesting and not what I had been used to. I was more accustomed to wondering hands, touching, even kissing and no idle chit-chat but he was very restrained and this time I limited my alcohol intake so I too was being more conservative.

Eventually as the evening drew to a close I asked him would he like to go upstairs to bed with me. He was delighted and probably waiting to be asked all night. I wasn't sure though as he had already fucked me and seen my boobs. Why would he want me again? I was thinking because most men I had been with around that time just had sex the once and moved on but he definitely wanted more.

I took him by the hand and led him to the room. We had, at that time, a special bedroom for entertaining so that we didn't use our own bed. I led him in, asked him to take off his shirt and sit on the bed and then told him I would get changed and come back. When I returned I was wearing a little cobalt blue silk nightie which just went below my bum, just enough to cover me as I wasn't wearing any pants. I had little cobalt silk knickers to match but figured I wouldn't be needing them. It had little shoulder straps holding it up but with no bra underneath so he could see the outline of my breasts and my nipples poking through it. I liked it because it felt nice against my skin and made me look and feel sexy.

He was still sitting there like a good boy when I entered, shirt off, as requested. He stood up as I walked over and I put out my hands to take his. I slid his hands around and onto my bum so that he knew I had no pants on and I felt him grope and cup my cheeks under the nightie.

As he did he let out a sigh. Maybe it was of relief, maybe happiness but whatever it was we didn't kiss!

I was looking down at first as I undid his belt and dropped his trousers to the floor. I hadn't seen his penis before although I had maybe touched it and I knew it had been inside me. We hadn't mentioned that when we chatted before but I knew it was him in bed with me that night.

I knew what he liked. I knew he liked to stare at my breasts so I asked him to lie on the bed. I sat next to him and began feeling his legs, my nails were painted red and he said he liked that but that was the only time he spoke. My hands drifted inside his boxers feeling around before sliding them off. I took his balls in my hand as I sat on him straddling him at his knees. I slid my hand up and down the shaft of his penis as my other hand slid up his chest and I remembered the slammer as I slid my finger inside his mouth. I knew he too was thinking about the salt as he sucked my finger. Before long I was sucking him, stopping at times to look up at him as he lay there motionless, hands at his side. I stopped before he got too excited and slid my body upwards so that my clitoris was resting on his penis which was still throbbing from my sucking. I slipped backwards and forwards as his penis shaft parted the lips of my clitoris and his expression changed as he felt the warmth inside me.

I would have usually put on a condom at this point but he'd already been inside me.

I knew he liked to stare at my boobs so before I let him inside this time I slowly slipped each strap over my shoulder allowing my nightie to fall to my waist and revealed to him my wonderful breasts. His hands were gently resting on my legs and he made no attempt to grab me or grope me as I arched my hips and slid my hand behind grabbing his balls at first and then his penis so that I could guide it inside. Once in place I slid down his shaft and watched as his head fell back into the pillow. Up and down I slid holding his chest for balance, sometimes slowly, sometimes bouncing fast as he watched my jiggling breasts. No touching, no kissing, just fucking. I was riding him, riding my husband's boss and I could hear laughter downstairs and remember hearing music drifting up. It was the Paula Cole song, *'I don't wanna wait'* blasting loudly from the stereo.

He continued to stare at me as he lifted his hands above his head. My hands slid from his chest up his arms and into his hands clenching our fists together as his body bucked up towards me and I arched in unison until he came. I fell to his side and turned to him, 'Do you want to feel my boobs?' I said and he nodded, smiling. I turned slightly with my back to him and took his right hand and placed in on my left boob at first and then across to the right so his arm was across me and he was holding my right breast tight in his hand. I then lifted my leg over his and pulled him into my crotch as he spooned me whilst feeling and groping me. I didn't know if he would be able to go on but I slid my hand between my legs and grabbed his still semi-hard penis which was getting harder as he groped my breasts for the first time. I pulled it hard up and down until it was hard enough to put inside me. We found each other so that he was again inside me spooning me as we lay together. I lay there enjoying him as he began to slide in and out with ease. I was wondering why he never kissed me; maybe he liked me too much? Maybe he was afraid of falling for me? As I lay there, feeling his breath on my neck, his arm across my chest and with his hand holding my breast, I had an orgasm. Not a thunderous orgasm but one with waves of intense pleasure and I'm sure he also came again, perhaps we even came together?

He must have because without a word he rose dressing himself, not frantically but quickly and quietly. I didn't turn and instead just lay there enjoying the feeling between my legs. It was just like it had been when I first had sex with my husband, as if there was a tiny vibrator still inside.

As he left the room I felt denied, denied my kiss. I like to snog when having sex. I like to feel someone's tongue inside me when they are inside me and I wanted to taste him. He had been inside me twice and yet we hadn't even kissed!

I let him leave and walk out the door. He didn't even say goodbye but as I lay there thinking about his lips I couldn't contain myself so I bounced up and dashed after him and when I got to the stop of the stairs he was half way down, 'Wait!' I called.

As he turned I was standing there completely naked in front of him, at the top of the stairs, with my hands out beckoning him to come to me. Thankfully he obliged but not until he had taken a moment to look me up and down and take in the sight before him.

He came to me, not all the way up but enough so that our heads were level. 'Kiss me', I said and as he leant in. I took his hands and again slid them behind me placing them back onto my cheeks and he held them just as he had when it had all started earlier. My mind and his raced back to that point playing the whole thing in flashes back in our minds as we stared at one another. It seemed like hours passed by before his lips finally touched mine. It was a gentle and dry kiss. He kissed me a couple of times but not passionately, not a wet kiss, more like a couple of long slow kisses on the lips then he turned and left.

He left me wanting more, left me wanting him, wanting his kiss, wanting him again, wanting him inside me once more but with his tongue in my mouth.

I went back to the bed we had been in before he left me and I lay there thinking about him most of that night and about how much I wanted him to kiss me, to take me and to come inside me, over and over again.

The next morning I knew my husband had enjoyed the two girls because they had made a bed on the living room floor and were a tangled mess of naked limbs when I arrived with their cups of coffee.

I only ever saw my husband's boss once more after that night. They parted ways when my husband moved jobs and as they no longer work in the same place it's unlikely our paths will ever cross again but that last time I saw him was amazing.

I was in town one day shopping and decided to surprise my husband and take him for lunch; I remember it was just after 1pm so I was in a rush hoping to catch him in the office.

When I arrived everyone had already gone to lunch but just as I turned to leave there he was, my husband's boss, standing in front of me. He said that my husband was at an early business lunch and would not be long and asked if I wanted to wait. I couldn't look him in the eye at first but he seemed more confident than ever before.

He brought me into his office to wait which was massive. It had a large window with two desks in an L shape in front of it and in the corner was what looked like the corner of a coffee shop with two big comfy leather sofas, a coffee table and a coffee machine on the side board. I accepted a coffee from him and he gestured for me to sit on the sofa. He sat beside me, really close, as close as he did the first night I met him in our house. There was plenty of room but he was so close my leg was touching his. I was wearing a denim shirt but without tights as it was May and the warm weather had arrived. I could feel the heat of his body coming into mine where we touched.

He seemed completely different though, much stronger. I was in his domain and he felt in control at last.

When I finished my coffee he took the empty cup from me and sat it on the table. We talked about the parties but not about the times he had been inside me. In fact we had never even discussed that first night when he came up to my bed. I wanted to ask him. I wanted him to know I knew about it, that I knew it was him but he seemed too powerful in his domain. I may have been a little scared as he looked at me different than before, not as the gentleman I knew but more so in a naughty or dirty way.

Although I may have been scared I was turned on thinking about him and I, as we chatted. His hand found my knee at the point where our knees met and then as he continued chatting his hand moved. His fingers slid slowly down and under my leg. His thumb, still on top of my leg, began moving backwards and forwards caressing my skin. As his hand inched upwards between my legs I couldn't help but look down at his hand as it began to tighten around my leg squeezing and groping rather than caressing. I hadn't noticed him slide his other arm behind me until it gripped my shoulder firmly and pulled me back deep into the sofa allowing his hand further up my leg until it was touching my inner thigh.

When I looked up at him he was close, his face very close to mine. Was he going to kiss me at last? I thought. Yes he did! but as his lips touched mine his hand reached my pants. I was lying back in the sofa with my husband's boss, his hand gripping my pants, his other hand now holding my head pushing it into him as he pushed his tongue inside, finally inside my mouth, licking me, snogging me!

I enjoyed his taste and I enjoyed his force as he took control and snogged me hard and harder. His hands were inside my pants and he was massaging my clitoris with his thumb before fucking me with his fingers, pushing in one then two at a time. My back arched as he thrust his fingers inside. I wanted him to enjoy me but I wanted him inside me in his office. My mind raced; would anyone come? What time was it? Was my husband due back? This was not right! I was thinking all these mad thoughts when I came. It was a different orgasm than before and much, much more powerful as the waves of excitement engulfed me. I didn't even know that my hand was between his legs holding his hard cock through his trousers. I didn't know what time it was as I closed my eyes and enjoyed the moment I kept them closed remembering the first time when my eyes were closed, that night in the bed and the whole time wondering what he was doing. As I pondered I realised his hand was no longer between my legs and his fingers no longer inside me.

They were unbuttoning my shirt. I felt the buttons pop as I still lay there, eyes still shut enjoying my orgasm and enjoying him kissing my neck. I was lying there lifeless just like the first time as he shuffled his hand inside my bra whilst his mouth and warm tongue licked my neck and then moved down my chest. I squeezed his dick hard in my hand as his mouth found my nipple licking it and flicking it with his tongue, sucking it hard. It was so sensitive I felt like I was going to explode.

I didn't know what to do, he was in control this time but again he got up quickly and quietly. I opened my eyes to see him standing in front of me as I fixed myself closing my legs and putting my breast back inside my bra. I glanced quickly at the clock behind him, nearly two o'clock I remember. I must get out of this office but he still had a determined look about him, was he not yet done?

I was! I was finished and in need of something, a drink, fresh air, maybe even a sleep but he was not finished, not yet. He unzipped his trousers and pulled out his cock which was still very erect. I was sitting in front of him with my hands and fingers shaking as I tried to button my shirt.

He leaned over and slid his fingers into my hair at either side of my head turning my face upwards to him and as we caught eye contact I could feel the force of his hands holding me hard and pulling me forward towards his cock. I knew what he wanted and I had got what I wanted. I had wanted that kiss. I didn't expect what came with it but I had longed for it and he knew it. He'd been inside me and came inside me before so this time he wanted me to take him in my mouth. He wanted to come inside me again, this time in my mouth.

I licked his shaft from bottom to top first making him shudder and loosen his grip on my head. My hands were still trying to button my shirt and still shaking as I was aware of the time and the need to get out of there. I began sucking him hard, harder and then harder, licking the tip and gulping down the shaft quickly then slowly rising each time beckoning the spunk to come with me. I kept on until it did the final time into my mouth and away when I swallowed.

As I stood his mood changed. He was no longer as forceful but back to that gentle man, that gentle man with a dirty wanting side, a side that could turn on intense need, greed even but it was now gone and his gentle nature came back to the surface as he leaned forward and buttoned my shirt for me. No words just a kind gesture. With my legs hardly holding me up I left him. The office was thankfully still empty and I remember kissing him on the cheek before I turned to go. I didn't wait around for my husband I just left. I didn't go shopping just went home and got into the bath and realised that's what I needed, a long hot soak.

For along time after that each time I had a bath I remembered my husband's boss.

Chapter Fourteen – The Photographer

We had made friends with lots of different people and our lives were the better for it. Our lives were enriched by the married and non-married couples we had shared and enjoyed spending time with both sexually and just having fun together. Our circle of friends grew wider with each passing month and as more time passed we were introduced to many different people from all walks of life.

It was a very interesting time for us both and as we had both enjoyed casual sex with others our own sex life became much more kinky and enjoyable. We would think nothing of sneaking off to the toilets in a restaurant to have sex or stopping at the side of the road during a long drive to fornicate or pleasure each other.

We were closer, much closer than before and I loved my husband. I had been with lots of other men but I loved my husband. It was never cheating to me as he knew about it so it was ok. I was happy being with these men safe in the knowledge he was nearby. The reality of it all was a far cry from what I imagined it to be. In reality I was cheating, I must have been because

I had encounters my husband didn't know about but then I questioned if he had done the same. It felt right, ok even, to me and before long it became a drug, a need to be desired and to be fucked by strangers. The need became a craving which would have to be satisfied at all costs. I knew that when I met the photographer.

We were on holiday, my husband and I with a group of friends staying in a nice resort. The holiday was all-inclusive so we stayed mainly within the complex. The resort was well known to people back home and many people came from where we lived to holiday there. So much so in fact that you would nearly always bump into someone you knew from back home or recognised. The night we met we were all having dinner together in one of the complex's many restaurants. It was late in the evening and the sun was setting over the bay glowing red like a large red ball in the sky. I watched as it dipped below the horizon as if it was sinking into the sea. The sea was calm but the gentle waves flickered red as the sun sank deeper into the water. At first my gaze was fixed on the sunset and I didn't notice him arrive at our table. He was a friend of one of the friends we were on holiday with. We were the youngest of the people we were away with and he too was about ten years my senior. He seemed to be alone and I felt him looking at me before I turned to see him myself. As the sun dipped out of sight I finally turned back to the table to join in the conversation which I had caught bits of as I watched my picture fade.

'Beautiful isn't it', were his first words to me as he realised I was turned enough to hear him. 'Yes' I replied focusing my eyes on who had spoken to me. He was standing and at the other side of the table from me, he continued, 'I have some fantastic pictures of the sunset here it is amazing'. 'He's a photographer' my friend said before I engaged in the chat, 'Are you here on holiday?' I queried. 'No I'm working' was his reply and that fascinated me.

This man was there at that beautiful time of year not to soak it up or even to sunbathe. He wasn't there to drink away his days or lounge by the pool. Instead he was there to capture its beauty and that made me very interested in him. He came around the table as the small talk continued and pulled up a chair beside me. He told me about where he had been and about the pictures he had taken and why he had chosen this area to capture. I was mesmerised by his stories and after a while I realised I had not been part of our group. I had instead spent all evening talking to this man, a stranger!

The way he described photography and the pictures of beauty he had seen turned me on. His understanding of nature and how important the world around us was made me feel sexually aroused. He was taller than me but only just. His hair had been black at one point in his life but was now almost grey, silver even. It was parted and pulled to one side as if it had been forced that way for years. His shirt was unbuttoned and his chest contained curly hairs a mixture of grey and black. He was fairly tanned although his face was more red than brown and his forehead, larger due to his age and receding hair line, was very red as if he had spent too long out in the sun talking his pictures.

He wasn't my type but his words were sensual and deep and the idea of his pictures was romantic. I asked him did he do portraits and the conversation soon turned to him talking pictures of me. I turned to my husband with this suggestion and he was very happy for me to be photographed. He wanted the pictures himself for his desk at work and thought it was a great idea. We then discussed technical matters like lighting and poses and his professional manner made me feel less aroused and more studious.

Later that night when we retired to the bar he brought us some of his albums. They contained tiny pictures about 24 to a sheet and were difficult at first to make out but he knew every detail recapturing the moment in his mind. As he described each moment the picture came alive almost enlarging itself as he spoke allowing me to imagine myself in the pic and I desperately wanted him to take my pics straight away. We agreed a time for the following day and I arranged to meet him in his apartment late afternoon. He said it would take him some time to set up the lights.

It took me longer to decide what to wear and in the end my husband chose a dress I had away with me. It was a long black dress. It plunged deep at the front and deeper at the back much like my purple one which I had left at home. The dress continued to the floor with a large split up the outside of the leg. It was very classy but light enough material to wear in the warm weather. I wore strappy, gold, metallic, high heel, dress sandals on my feet but left off my jewellery.

It was hot that day and he had arranged the shoot for

late afternoon so that most of the heat from the day would be disappearing as the sun began to set over the sea.

When I first knocked on his door he was still mucking around with lights but as I walked around his apartment he lifted his camera and started snapping asking me to keep walking as if I had moved exactly how he wanted me too. It was very hot in his apartment and the doors to the balcony were wide open. Most of the heat inside was coming from the lighting he had rigged up. He was sweating buckets and in the end had to remove his shirt. He apologised as he removed it unable to contend with the heat but I didn't care. He seemed to wonder how I could still look so perfect in the heat as he told me to stand out on the balcony and he continued snapping away with his camera.

He asked me to look out over the sea as the sun came down and I'm sure he hoped the heat would die down with it. He was snapping me from behind as the outline of my bum was clear for him to see and I'm sure he realised I had no underwear on. My arms were crossed and my hands loosely holding the railing. I got turned on as he got closer imaging the railing was his hard penis as I held it tight sometimes sliding my hand along it. I could tell he was watching it as he leant in to take some close ups of my face against the setting sun. My nails were perfectly manicured and I wondered if he was thinking what I was thinking?

As he came closer asking me to turn my head he seemed taken aback once more by my beauty remarked at how I looked through his lens. His breath becoming more like a pant as I swayed my head side to side for him, smiling at him in a sexy way. I could feel the heat from the sun on the side of my face as the fading light touched only one side, perfect he said as he loomed even closer to capture the shot. He pulled back around me taking pictures behind me and I was sure he was zooming in on the curves of my backside.

I too was getting hot, remembering how he described his pictures but also at his closeness and his close examination of me. All over me his eyes and camera lens were and I felt hotter inside as well as outside. He asked me to turn once more and I felt the heat touch my breast. The entire side of each breast was exposed by the dress and the light warmed my breast and turned it pink. He watched as the sunlight crept onto my cleavage like a warm red hand and I wondered if he wanted to swap places with it. As the sunlight hit my curves and he continued to snap away I could see now how interested he was in me by the bulge appearing in his shorts. He knew the light was fading and needed me inside but it was warmer inside and the lights would be glaring so he took his time, enough to savour the moment but then he and I both wanted more. He wanted more pics, more flesh. I wanted more too but did we want the same thing?

He was so close to me I could imagine him reaching out to touch my breast and I hoped he was thinking the same as he asked me to go back inside. I walked to him and then past him and his hand came up and rested in the curve of my spine gently touching my lower back as we walked into the room together. I wanted his hand to slide down my curves and grab my behind but it didn't.

I wondered was he showing restraint or if I was reading the situation wrongly.

Back inside the room I asked, 'Do you want me on the bed?' hoping to ignite his seemingly obvious desire to bed me. Wiping the sweat from his brow as he struggled for the words to say I imagined his answer, hoping that it would be dirty, willing it to be. Instead it was a simple, 'Yes' followed by, 'If you could lean back with your arms behind you and tilt your head that would be great'.

I did as he asked and as I sat back I crossed my legs so that the dress would fall at the split revealing my whole leg right to the top, 'Perfect' he said as he continued to snap, zooming in on my leg as the camera pointed downwards. I flicked my head from side to side to shake the hair from my face as the camera lifted and seemed to zoom once again to my breast as the dress held it in place, just! I wanted his hand to be there and as I watched him he licked his lips. Perhaps he was licking the sweat away but to me he was thinking about licking my nipples. I was getting more and more horny and wanted sex so bad.

He then asked, 'Can we try some different shots?' to which I thought, yes this is it! He will want me out of this dress and so I replied, 'Ok, do you want me to change?' He gulped and the gulp in his throat seemed to prevent him from answering so I stood up from the bed, close to him and turned my back to him, 'Can you unzip me?' Again without a word he set down the camera and this time did as I asked until my dress fell to the floor leaving me wearing only my gold strappy sandals.

He could see my body from behind, completely naked and I could see his reflection in the mirror as his eyes wandered up and down before fixing his gaze on my backside. I hoped he would grab it but he didn't. His eyes were then drawn to the mirror I was looking at and he could see the outline of my body, my silhouette and the side of my breast. He seemed to be taking photos in his mind of my naked body, hoping to remember what he was seeing, wishing he could snap me naked or better still touch me!

I wanted him to touch me and feel me all over. I wanted him to enjoy me in the way he enjoyed all his subjects. I wanted him to think of this and play it over in his mind just as he did those sunsets and the other pictures which he described so beautifully to me recalling the moment forever in his mind. I knew he was by then dying to touch me too, to feel me, to see my breasts in full so I put my hands behind my back beckoning him to come to me.

Reading the situation, at last, he put his hands into mine and I pulled him closer. His eyes that had been transfixed on the mirror after seeing only the side of my breast were now looking down on both of them over my shoulder and I felt his breath deepen on my neck as I took his hands around my waist and placed them onto my breasts. My nipples were erect as he held them gently at first before groping them harder and harder and as he himself became harder and harder. I passed my hands once again behind me unbuttoning his shorts and letting them fall to the floor at his ankles. Stood there in that clinch was like the time my husband and I first had sex, holding each other in the same way but the photographer was less relaxed and I was in full control. I knew exactly what I was doing. It wasn't romantic, it wasn't love, it was sex I wanted, pure and simple.

I tilted my head back towards him with my hands inside his boxers.

As my hands slid up and down his shaft he seemed unable to let go of my breasts; the ones he had watched, the ones I knew he had wanted and waited for but I wanted more. As the breeze began to flow through the open door to cool our bodies I turned to him and asked him to turn off the camera lighting knowing that we needed more cool air if we were to get any more excited and hoping the dimmer light would make him more adventurous.

He turned away from me to turn off the lights and as he did I came up behind him so that he could feel my erect nipples on his back, sliding down his back as I dropped to my knees taking his boxers down with me. He was standing naked, the lights finally off and the fading sunlight over the ocean giving an orange, warming glow to his front as I slid my hands up his legs.

He knew what was to happen next and for the first time he knew what to do so he turned to me allowing the glow to warm his back as my hands slid all over his legs finding themselves in between. He was looking down at me as I concentrated on his cock cupping his balls in my hand and licking wildly, my tongue lashing in and out over his balls. He sighed in delight as I licked his shaft from bottom to top with my other hand reaching around and holding his bum. Again he seemed to be taking mental photos, trying not to come, trying not to explode in my face but wanting to, dying to at the same time.

I put his cock in my mouth still holding his balls in one hand whilst the other slid up his chest until he grabbed it, hoping this would never end but knowing it would and holding my hand tight so that I could not escape the moment.

He told me afterwards that as I sucked and sucked he remembered the beginning of the photo shoot, playing it again in his mind from the start until that point and when he got to that part and he could feel my tongue lashing the tip of his penis he could hold back no more as he came onto my face, hoping again that it wasn't the end of our encounter.

Of course it wasn't to be as I too needed the same treatment. I needed him to make me come, that's why I went there, to have him inside me. When he realised I needed more he became more relaxed and having come himself he wanted to kiss me. We hadn't yet kissed and he was thinking about how he wanted to taste me.

I lay back on the bed beckoning him to come and lie beside me. His hands felt me all over and he seemed unable to stop touching and caressing my curves as he leant over to finally kiss me but I turned away letting him only kiss my neck. This made him nervous, why weren't we kissing? Why didn't I let him? Reading his thoughts I said, 'Not yet' and I took his hand and placed it between my legs. It was time for him to return the favour and as he grabbed and groped between my legs he was still looking over every inch of my naked body and taking more mental photos. His eyes were saying, I want you, I want to eat you and as I got wetter he slid his hand up and down my clitoris, teasing me and kissing my neck again before flicking his finger inside for a second. As I shuddered waiting for it again his mouth found its way down to my breasts sucking and licking my nipples then another flicker inside then another before they became longer, harder, pushing in and out, two fingers then went inside. His hands were caressing me everywhere. His mouth kept going downwards until he was kissing my belly and licking around my belly button.

There was still no snogging but what his mouth was doing was better. It was fantastic. I was getting tingles all over my body and pulling him closer. He was nearly on top of me and by then he was getting hard again, ready again as I felt his penis dig into my leg. His head got even lower until he replaced his fingers with his tongue. My head went backwards as his tongue penetrated me and he remembered the pictures of me on the bed, my back arching as he lashed out with his tongue and also dug fingers in deep pulling me upwards with his strength until finally I pulled him up toward me, pulling him into me, closer still, digging my nails into his back as I came, moaning loudly with his fingers still inside.

My face was turned to the side, his body on top of mine

with his face buried in my neck. His cock was stiffening as my body relaxed and my legs opened wider allowing him to fall in between them. His penis was touching my soaking wet vagina, feeling it wet and warm against the tip of his shaft. I wanted him inside and I knew he wanted it too but as I lay there completely relaxed beneath him he seemed to be questioning, could he do it? Should he do it?

I needed him inside me, I wanted him inside. I willed it but did he want to? Did he know I wanted him to?

The tension mounted as the moment grew in time and stature.

I then turned my head to his as all his muscles contorted, willing him to push forward and into me. I could feel the tip of his penis touching the lips of my clit as they parted easily beckoning him inside. I could feel his muscles tight at the bottom of his back as I ran my hands down either side of his spine resting at the small of his back as I writhed beneath him, moaning, groaning with pleasure and intent.

I looked right at him and as we stared at one another I said, 'Kiss me'

His back relaxed slightly and his body relaxed as he gently laid it on top of mine. He was no longer holding his penis at the entrance to me but resting it on top of my vagina, resting his body, no longer tensing his muscles as his face closed in on mine. He looked into my eyes as his face came forward to mine then his eyes glanced down at my lips to find the target. Finally I let his lips touch mine, gently at first as he held my head in his hand before snogging me. I could feel his penis throbbing against my clitoris and I ached to have him inside.

We kissed and snogged and licked each other getting faster and more furious as our tongues lashed one another's. We panted as we attempted to catch our breath and as we frantically kissed our bodies both tensed in frustration again.

His hand found my breast and my hands his bare bum squeezing him closer so I could feel his hard shaft against me once again before I finally pulled my head back away from his stopping the kissing so our eyes met once more. With his hand still holding my breast. I looked straight at him again and then I said, 'Fuck me!'

After the holiday we kept in touch. I had given him my email address so he could send the pictures to me and, as promised, I gave my husband some. The pictures on the balcony were terrific and I felt like a model. We chatted by email and at first it was just to talk about what happened but then we began to talk dirty to one another. I looked forward to his emails and he enjoyed my equally dirty replies. I was finding myself getting horny in work as we talked about what we wanted to do to each other and where we might do it.

I had been promoted and was doing the job my husband did originally when we first met. I had my own office (his old office) and more time on my hands. I looked forward to going in each morning and checking my mail and spending lunchtime locked away in the office dreaming up dirty sexy scenarios for us to write about. I no longer watched the porn DVDs my husband made but instead I got my kicks from my email exchanges at work. When I used my vibrator I no longer thought about my husband or the porn I had seen as I had my own experiences to recall and hoped I would have many more to come.

I remembered things I had done and imagined things I wanted to do. I then emailed my thoughts and plans to the photographer. We chatted about porn and about how he always wanted to photograph it. We talked about two men and me and how he would love to capture that. His studio was on the other side of the city so when he began to plan it the reality that it might actually happen hit me. I was nervous at first but then excited. He told me he could hire two porn actors and sent me pictures to choose from. In the end I let him pick them. The night before I lay awake imagining what it might be like and I wasn't disappointed.

I arrived at his studio and he had the two guys waiting for me. I kissed him at the door when I arrived and he grabbed my ass as we kissed. He was no longer the shy man I met on holiday. He then took my hand and led me to an area which looked like a living room and I sat on the sofa between the two guys who handed me a glass of wine. As I sipped the drink he got the camera ready studying what I was wearing, a short denim skirt, a simple white t-shirt and a denim jacket along with my little strappy sandals I wore for him that night on holiday.

He looked at me and said, 'Would you like to take off your jacket?' and as I stood to do so I placed my wine on the table and his snapping began. With the camera clicking each guy took a leg and began to run their hands up and down as he leaned it for close ups and took my jacket from me. I had no bra on and my nipples are erect and inviting, so much so he couldn't resist and he felt my left breast before sitting back in his chair.

One of the guys stood beside me as I winced and moaned because the other already had his hand inside my skirt. We hadn't even been introduced and his hands were on my pants. The guy standing was then kissing me when his hand slid inside my top feeling me everywhere. He then guided my top up over my head and for a brief moment I paused as the photographer snapped my bare breasts with his camera. I then noticed my skirt was around my ankles as the guy on the sofa was taking it off over my strappy heels.

'Why don't you sit down?' said the photographer and as I sat back on the sofa I was naked and had one guy at each side of me so I slid my legs open wide and placed them on top of their legs. I took each of their cocks in my hands. The one that had been standing was rock hard as he continued to play with my breasts and kiss my neck. The other was softer at first but as I rubbed him he got harder and he too began kissing me, licking and flicking my tongue with his whilst sliding his hand between my legs feeling my warm, wet pussy.

The other guy was sucking on my nipples and I wanted to come, to scream! I looked at my photographer as if to say, I can't take this! I wanted him inside me, the photographer, someone familiar. I had no idea what would happen next and felt out of control as these young men's hands were all over me. One of them settled between my legs and his fingers lashed in and out of me, furiously in and out of my pussy. The guys then switched and the hand that had been inside me came out just as I was about to orgasm. It then came up to my mouth letting me taste its fingers before touching my breasts. That was his first feel of my breast and he grabbed it differently than the other, much more firm. He grabbed it even harder when I pulled hard on his penis. His had been the softer of the two before but by then he was pulsating. I concentrated on him as I let the other penis go and he stood up from the sofa. Still standing he lifted my body up so I was on all fours on the sofa and still holding the other penis in my grasp. The guy standing then began to tongue me from behind as I sucked hard on the penis I had been holding and the guy it belonged to lay back looking like he was ready to come.

He started to recoil and I knew he was going to come; I stopped for a second and looked over to the photographer who was playing with himself. I took his cock again in my mouth and swallowed as he came into my mouth but then I thought, what's going on? I felt my body shove forcefully forward as the other guy entered me, WOW! The other guy was inside me taking me hard from behind. I had been too busy concentrating on the other and it took me by surprise.

So much so that I came myself and as I orgasmed over and over the guy below me sucked hard on my nipples and the other banged me from behind slapping my ass and groping my legs.

The photographer then came over slipping his hand under my body to cup my breast whilst still snapping with his camera and with his cock out and hard. I slid my hands up and down it as the force of the fuck from behind continued to shove me backwards and forwards. As the other guy finished off all over my back I finally rose from the sofa, weak at the knees and naked in front of them all.

I wasn't finished though, I still wanted more so I took the photographer's cock in my hand and led him into the bedroom.

I never saw either of those guys again but I did go back to the photographer's to look at the photographs and fuck him again.

We were sitting together on that sofa and looking at the pics he had taken on sheets which were on my lap. He hovered, half behind and half beside me, as we both gazed at my naked body and the young men who were touching me. He told me that he had used the pictures to masturbate over and over again since printing them out. I hadn't intended to shag him when I agreed to go back again but when I saw the snaps I became rather randy and seeing that in my face and along with the photographer's newly found confidence he wasted no time in sliding his hands around my waist to grope me.

I sifted through the sheets of snaps with the photographer's hands feeling me through my blouse. I wanted to take the pics and run. I wanted to show my husband but I knew I couldn't. I wanted him to be involved in what I had done, what I was up to but I knew I couldn't tell him. The photographer's hand slipped inside my blouse and with one swift movement circled down into my bra and under my breast. He groped me and kissed my neck just like he had done when we first had sex but I didn't want him. I had already had him and although he still wanted me I wanted something more. The fire inside me had been lit and I wanted to feed it. I wanted sex but not with anyone I had been with before. More sex with strangers, more sex with two strange guys, that's what I want, I thought when my blouse was removed.

The pictures turned me on but he didn't as he removed my bra exposing my chest to him once again.

He pushed me back onto the sofa and I dropped my pictures. He carefully removed my shoes, then my trousers, then my pants and then he entered me.

I lay on the sofa trying to imagine he was the guys I had in me before but as I lay there and he satisfied himself inside me I began to wonder how I could get my next fix.

We continued to email for a while after that until I got bored with him. My urge to be fucked had grown greater. I wanted strangers and I wanted it all the time. My husband knew nothing about the photographer or the photos and that seemed to make it more exciting. I knew I needed another fix and then one day I found where to get it;

The internet.

Chapter Fifteen – The Internet

After a while the urge became a need, a want. I wanted sex, not just sex but sex with a stranger, someone new and different. No strings fun was what I was after and I didn't care how I got it. I had moved on from swinging I wanted more danger and more mystery. I wanted to feel like I did with the guy at my house when he fucked me on the kitchen counter or like I did with my husband's boss and perhaps I even wanted or needed to do it behind my husband's back.

Would he mind? I pondered but then dismissed the thought straight away in case I didn't like the answer. 'Probably not' I told myself instead, without really questioning my actions or thinking too much about it. After being with the photographer I knew what I wanted and that was to meet up with someone and have sex, but how? Was it to be that easy? Before then it had been set up at parties and usually by my husband so I was thinking, could I really do this alone, by myself?

I asked myself these questions over and over and began finding myself flirting in the most unusual places; with the bank teller at the bank, in a taxi, with the hairdresser even but that wasn't gonna lead to sex, not to one-time-only, no-strings-attached, sex.

I must have oozed sex appeal as I tarted myself up everywhere I went willing a man to jump me. I became desperate until I finally found an outlet, the internet.

A wonderful tool for my sexual desires I used dating and social networking sites to chat dirty to strangers which got me really excited and turned on. I would post my pictures and they would drool over them some did unspeakable things to them but it made me feel wanted and sexy.

I got many, many offers for sex and I was able to pick and choose who I would meet and when. Some were timewasters of course but one guy stood out from the rest. He was from London so I didn't think we would ever enjoy a full encounter but he sent me naked pictures of himself and I returned the favour. It was fun and exciting but harmless until the messages became more personal and we discussed our lives, where we worked, etc, etc. One day an envelope arrived on my desk and when I opened it there was a plane ticket inside. No Easyjet cheap flight but first class to London. It took me by surprise but it was for the following Friday and it was a flight in the morning and a return that afternoon.

It would mean taking the day off work but I could be there and back without anyone noticing I was gone. Would that be wise? I asked myself, going to meet a stranger in London god knows where and without anyone knowing I had gone or where I would be?

Then I thought, fuck it, you only live once!

As I boarded the plane I began to imagine what it would be like, to meet this stranger and bed him then fly home. I imagined it would be like that Boxing Day with my husband as we went to the hotel room. I imagined we would feel each other and be together for ages satisfying one another before making love. I imagined a scene very like that Boxing Day in the hotel room with my husband but the reality was very different.

We met in the hotel bar and he was waiting on me. As I arrived he stood to welcome me, kissing me on the cheek and groping my ass. He was not a gentleman like my husband and I guessed it was going to be different as he immediately began talking about sex. His hands wandered up and down my inner leg and I suddenly became aware of everyone around me, 'You have a room booked?' I asked finishing my drink. 'Of course' he replied as he pulled out the key card from his pocket as if it was a trophy of some kind. We went to the room, went inside and he immediately pounced on me pulling at my clothes to get me naked. I helped him so that they didn't get destroyed in the process. He fumbled with his own clothes but I didn't help him, instead I lay on the bed waiting for him. He put on his own condom and was stiff as a board when he mounted me.

He fucked me, grunting, as I took his weight on top of me. It was so different than my Boxing Day and so different than the way I had played it in my head. I enjoyed it though because by then I just loved having sex. I enjoyed not knowing what to expect and how to behave. I let him kiss me but it was forced and no real snogging took place. There was no romantic moment, no tenderness just a simple fuck. Perhaps that was what I should've expected. He was nice to me though and afterwards we chatted for a bit before parting company.

On the flight home I felt a little disappointed but instead of thinking I would not do that again I thought the opposite. I thought I must do that again and I will keep doing it until I find my perfect moment. I wanted to feel just like I did that Boxing Day, making love to a man for the first time.

And so I did it again and again. I became more adventurous meeting people anywhere, everywhere. I didn't care who they were or what they looked like as long as they were available. I wasn't choosy and that meant many weirdoes. Some people didn't turn up, some were even too afraid to go through with it but many, many others were just as dirty and as needy as me.

I remember meeting a man in his office. He invited me round at lunch time and I went there pretending to meet him on official business.

I knew nothing about him really other than what he looked like and what turned him on. I wore a short black pencil skirt and black stockings. I had a white blouse on with a black lace bra. I'm sure people in my own office could see the black bra through my blouse but I didn't care and to be honest I enjoyed the attention. I painted my nails black (as he had requested) and when

I arrived he made me a coffee. His office was small and compact, just him, his desk and a filing cabinet beside the door. I sat on the edge of his desk hitching my skirt up so he could see my stockings. We talked dirty as we sipped our coffee. He stretched out his hand to feel my stocking and remarked on my black nails. He then got up and came round in front of me parting my legs and sliding his hands up the inside of my legs. He made his way inside my pants and flicked me with his fingers while he stared into my eyes.

I asked to him to fuck me but he pointed to the door and showed me that people could see in so he told me to go and lean against the filing cabinet beside the door so that no-one could see. I did what he asked and as he approached me I unbuttoned my blouse. His eyes lit up as I unveiled my chest. He licked his lips before shoving his hands down my bra and pulling out my breasts. His body lunged forward pressing mine against the cabinet and his hands fumbled about up inside my skirt. He pulled aside my pants and put on his condom before shoving his cock into me, fucking me hard up against the cabinet. He kissed my neck but not my lips or face. He then buried his head in my neck and fucked me hard all the time pressing my body into the cold hard metal of the cabinet. It was over quick and as he came he pulled away releasing the pressure on my body. He looked into my eyes and groped my tits for a bit while grunting before walking away, back behind his desk and sitting down. I fixed myself and left.

And so it continued like that and becoming the norm. I would start by chatting on the internet to strangers, then exchange pics, arrange a meet and then have sex before deleting the contact details and never speaking to them ever again. I had no shame and was happy to show them pictures of my pants or my nipples or indeed anything they asked for.

The desire to continue was the craving that I couldn't control and I gave myself to many men during that time without considering the consequences or even if I fancied them.

My favourite though came as a surprise. It was a young farmer that caught my interest. His fantasy was to have sex in one of the barns on his father's farm and this appealed to me so as soon as Spring arrived I arranged to meet him.

The day we met was the first week of a hot spell. The sky was blue interspersed only with fluffy white clouds like cotton wool dotted here and there. I remembered the car journey as I drove to our meeting place. I was listening to The Fray, *'How to save a life'* and singing it loudly and badly as I drove along with the air-con on full whack.

When I arrived he was stood there at the side of the road waiting. We had been texting each other as I neared my destination so I could find the right spot and so he knew when I'd arrive.

He was younger than me but still in his twenties. He was fit and wearing a red checked shirt with the sleeves ripped off. His arms were muscley and sexy and I thought I would enjoy having them wrapped around me. I had seen his body before in the pics he had sent me but it was even more delicious in the flesh.

I parked the car beside him and got out. My nipples which were hard from the cool air-conditioned air in the car drew his gaze towards them as we exchanged pleasantries, mostly about the fine weather.

He then took my hand and we walked along a gravelled path which became a dusty track of mud cracked hard by the Spring sunshine. As we got closer to the barn his grip on my hand tightened in anticipation of what was to come.

We entered the barn still hand in hand and both aware of what was going to happen but not knowing how or when it would. He picked the spot and sat down patting the hay next to him for me to sit down too. I was wearing my short denim skirt and a green vest top and he knew from the nipple incident I wasn't wearing a bra. He stared at my top and I knew he wanted to get his hands inside it. Sure enough as I sat next to him my chest was his first target as he leant over to kiss me.

My knees were up at first so he slid his hand behind them and around my waist, under my boobs feeling the underside of them as his arm slid round.

He kissed me softly at first putting me at ease allowing my legs to drop thus giving him more room to manoeuvre his hand up inside my top. Our tongues lashed against one another much faster than at first and his hand found its way well inside my top. I could feel it slightly cool against my skin making me aware of its movement as he felt my side at first, slowly inching upwards towards the prize.

As the kissing became snogging it became wet and wild and I felt my hand rise up to his check almost pulling his face closer, pulling him into my mouth. It was then I felt his thumb stroke my breast backwards and forwards as his hand slowly found its way, finding the nipple and finally cupping my breast. He spent time gently squeezing and groping, happy to have his hand there at last after months of looking at my pictures. I pulled him harder toward me until I fell back sinking into the hay and taking him with me. He was still supporting his weight on his other elbow as he started to grab at my breast and then his hand went away but straight across to my other breast, his touch much warmer than before. He massaged my breast gently at first until he started grabbing again as his body began arching towards me. I could feel his hardness rubbing my leg as I sat up to push him off.

'Have I gone too quick?' he said before realising I was pulling my top off over my head. As he stared at my perfect breasts I could see how much he wanted them but before he could touch them again I began unbuttoning his jeans sliding my hand inside to reveal his hardness to me. He helped by removing his jeans and once we were both half naked I lay back again pulling him onto me. His hands wandered, his mouth wandered too as it kissed and tasted all over my torso. My hand was on his pulsating penis when he started sucking my nipples and then slid his hand up my skirt. I felt his body sigh as he realised I wasn't wearing any pants! He began rubbing me at first then fingering me before taking off my skirt gently down my legs leaving me lying naked in the hay.

I unbuttoned his shirt as he put on his condom revealing his six pack and sexy pecs. Once he had put his condom on I pulled him once more on top of me and both of us were then naked in the hay.

I ran my hands up and down his back grabbing his ass pulling him towards me and then; he penetrated me. His penis was large and throbbing as its force entered my body then eased as he pulled back, almost out, before coming back inside deeper and then again harder and harder as my head fell back into the hay. He kissed and sucked my neck, fucking me, fucking me…. until he was ready to come.

He pulled out and removed the condom and burst his come out onto my breasts.

As I lay there in the hay covered in his sperm and looking up at him with the summer sun streaming through the barn silhouetting his fit body I thought to myself;

Best picture ever!

My photographer would have loved to be here right now to see this!

Chapter Sixteen - The Villa

A group of us went on holiday to a villa we had rented for a week in Spain. It was a remote location with not much night life about the place but still with plenty of local bars and restaurants and the all important ingredient for a sun lover like me, tanning time!

My husband and I went with his sister and her friend. His sister's boyfriend was going too along with her friend's husband. They were all a bit older than us and I guess I was probably the youngest there but only by a few years. We all had a similar idea of a relaxing holiday and were happy enough to laze about during the day and then relax over a long evening meal each night with plenty of wine and beer to keep everyone happy. That's why we booked a villa holiday and as it was a large one we all had our own bedrooms. Ours had an en-suite while the other two couples shared a bathroom.

We arrived first and so picked our room as we waited on the others who had travelled together. I knew his sister but her boyfriend was new so I had only met him a couple of times. I knew her friend better as we had all been out together before on a few girly nights but as they arrived that was the first time I had met her husband.

He checked me out over the top of his sunglasses and I could see his eyes run up and down me. He was nothing special, a man in his thirties with a receding hair line and thin lips. The rest of his face was covered by his large sunglasses but I noticed his pot belly as he bent down to lift the suitcases, however, what I noticed most was the colour of his skin. Like me he had olive skin, well tanned and I reckoned he too would be a sun worshipper.

I was right. There he was on the first morning out on the sun lounger even before me. The rest of the gang lay in their beds for what seemed like hours each day as we both caught the early morning rays. On that first day I could see his eyes again checking me out and following my hands as I rubbed tanning lotion onto my arms and legs. We never really said much other than 'Hello' or 'G'morning' and the usual small talk such as, 'Hot today isn't it?'

The others came out closer to lunchtime and we played games together such as volleyball in the pool and generally had a laugh.

The same routine continued for the first few days but the when we came back to the villa on the third night after once again being out in the local village the others stayed up for drinks but I went on to bed so I could get up early and catch the morning rays again. He also had the same idea and said 'G'night' to me as he passed, 'See you in the morning' I said with a smile but before

I ambled on to my bed he leant over and kissed me on the cheek and as he did so he took my hand briefly in his. That was the first time he kissed me, touched me even but not the last.

The next morning I was there first, Ha Ha, I thought, I've made it out before him! We exchanged the usual pleasantries and that was that. The difference that day though was that it was even later again before the others arrived and as I lay there I began to feel uneasy. I could tell he was staring at me again even though I couldn't see his eyes through his large dark sunglasses but it looked like he was also playing with himself behind his magazine and although I wondered what he was thinking I said nothing.

The following day when I arrived at my sun-lounger he had beaten me there again and was sitting all smug drinking coffee. He remarked on my tan and we discussed sunbathing for about ten minutes until I realised I had no sun lotion with me. As we were casually chatting I let him know and he immediately said I could use his. I turned to sit on the lounger and he rose from his seat with the lotion in his hand. I sat back into the lounger lifting my legs up onto it and he sat beside my legs facing me.

'I'll put it on for you' he said and started squeezing some into his hand. I never spoke and he proceeded to rub the lotion onto my thighs.

I lay back, becoming more relaxed, as he casually rubbed the lotion into my legs. He did not go too close to my bikini so I was happy to let him continue realising that it was lazy of me but not caring as it was saving me from having to do it.

He tickled my feet as he finished my legs and I winced as it tingled up my leg, 'Sorry' he remarked and stood up. I thought I had embarrassed him so I said, 'It was just tickly' but he didn't get up because of that and he was already moving around behind me. He then placed his hands on my shoulders and began once again rubbing lotion into my skin. He kinda massaged my shoulders as he rubbed and that relaxed me even more. As he rubbed my chest I was half expecting him to grope me and slide his oily hand inside my bikini. I was so relaxed I didn't care and my mind drifted back to the footie match at home and the time I was groped like this from behind but he didn't go there. His hands shook slightly as he dared to go near but not too close until he finally began rubbing my arms.

He sat down again beside my legs again as he finished by rubbing my hands. He said he thought I had lovely hands and loved my nail polish which pleased me as I had my nails done for going away. It was really nice having him play with my fingers as he slid his oily fingers in and out of mine. I knew he enjoyed it also because he had a lump in his shorts when he attempted to stand up. 'Thanks' I said as he lay back onto his own lounger next to mine.

The rest of that day was much like the others before. We all had some fun together when everyone finally got up although that night we stayed at the villa and had a barbeque. The boys all went off to the shops for more drink and to get the food and the girls stayed behind to start drinking.

I was already tipsy when they came back and by the time they had cooked the food and I finally had something to eat I was drunk. Not fall over drunk but talking rubbish drunk and really enjoying myself. The party rolled on and on and the gang started drifting off to bed, first his sister then her boyfriend. We tried keeping the barbeque lit to provide some heat after the sun had disappeared for good but by then I was beginning to shiver. My husband spotted this and threw me a blanket before heading off to bed himself.

My fellow sun worshipper saw this and took the opportunity to get under the covers with me stating he too was freezing and blaming our sun loving for us being so cold. He sat next to me and squeezed right up beside me. It was patio furniture we were on so it wasn't that big anyway but I could feel his body pressing against mine. There we were squeezed into a seat that only two small children would be comfortable together on and draped in a blanket as we both shivered and I continued to talk to his wife. The heat of his body against mine was a welcome change from the cool air and as his wife didn't seem to mind I became quite relaxed with him so close to me.

As the night rolled on more and more drink flowed and whilst the others had faded I decided to remain there and party on with my new friend, still keeping me warm under the blanket. His wife sat opposite us at the table seemingly happy at him and I together and keeping warm. It must've been pretty late or rather early the next day whichever way you look at it because the sky was beginning to lighten turning from a dark black to a silvery blue.

At one point while I was chatting to his wife and gossiping on about the latest celebrity news I felt a warm hand brush my thigh. It was very warm and the heat was welcome but when it happened again I began to feel uneasy as I wasn't sure if she saw the blanket move. Then it happened again but that time touching my leg. I put my hand down under cover to push his hand away but he grabbed my hand. There was nothing I could do. I was afraid to say anything and his hand was warm so I let him hold onto mine. He caressed my fingers like before and it was nice. He held my hand in a very caring gentle but sensual way as he stroked my hand he kept pulling it closer to him.

We were all chatting and I was fretting about what could be seen as the blanket moved then without warning my hand was pulled sharply toward him and my fingers prized open. Then they was closed around what I know now was his hard penis. It was very hot and very hard. I was embarrassed and I'm sure I was red in the cheeks but he kept my hand there and started masturbating using my hand as if it were is.

This went on for several minutes before he came all over my hand. I didn't know what to do or were to put my hand so I kindly rubbed it onto his shorts and pulled it away.

I was glad his wife hadn't seemed to notice what had occurred under the blanket and before long she too yawned, 'I'm off to bed' and it was only the two of us left, still huddled together, under there. I waited while she trotted off so I could confront him but as soon as his wife had disappeared out of sight he started whispering, 'Kiss me' in my ear and 'I want to fuck you… lets go into the pool now?', I was so drunk that my anger began to subside as his dirty thoughts poured into my ear through his warm breath which trickled down my neck and aroused me but I pulled myself together and said 'No way, I'm going to bed'. I was still annoyed at him taking liberties with my hand.

I stumbled as I tried to stand and he caught me, 'Come on, just one kiss?' 'A goodnight kiss that's all.' His face was so close to mine and he was trying to get his lips onto mine. 'No' I said once more as I broke free and began to walk away. I went into the kitchen for a drink of water and as I opened the fridge door with my right hand his hand appeared on top of mine holding it firmly and pushing the door shut. His body leant into my back before his other hand slid around my waist holding me just under my breasts. For a moment I felt like turning to him, kissing him and asking him to fuck me there and then on the kitchen bench but he ruined the moment when shoved his hand down the front of my skirt and the shock sobered me for a minute. 'Hey!' I said, 'that's enough.' He got the message and pulled back saying 'Sorry' and holding his hands up in a surrendering gesture but as I looked at him I remembered his gentle touch and his previous apology. He was a nice man, I thought, just obnoxious when drunk so I walked over to him and said, 'Just a goodnight kiss then'.

I titled my head and leaned into him and we snogged, gently at first and for what seemed like five long sensual minutes before he started getting frisky again. His hand grabbed at my bum then with one swift movement went down then up under my skirt. 'That's enough now, I'm going to bed' and off I went pushing him off me with both my hands and then staggering back to my room occasionally bouncing off the walls as I tried in vain to walk in a straight line.

The next morning was very different than all the others. I woke at mid-day with a sore head and with thoughts of the previous evening dancing around in my mind. At first I couldn't lift my head from the pillow and merely opening my eyes to let in the brightness of the day seemed such an arduous task. When I finally did, however, I noticed the time. I went into the kitchen to get headache tablets and noticed there was no-one about, no-one at the pool even. A note sat beside the kettle from my husband read;

Gone for lunch XX

No early morning sun today I thought as I jumped into the shower. I was enjoying my time in the shower in our en-suite when I heard the door, 'Is that you love?' I said but the voice that replied wasn't my husbands, it was him. 'You slept in too then?' it questioned.

'Yeah' I replied, 'The others are all away' he said. 'Back soon though' I said 'No' he replied 'they only left ten minutes ago'.

Shit! I thought this is a bit weird anyway I'm not going to let him bother me, 'Hand me the towel' I said and in it came through the curtain. He didn't peek in to my surprise as his eyes had scanned my entire body so many times I thought he would surely try for another.

I dried off and wrapped the towel around me hooking it in at my upper back. I knew my might be on show but I didn't care.

We chatted briefly about the night before skirting around the issues of the wank and the kiss but as I leaned into the mirror to fix my make up I could see him staring at my bum at it peaked out from below the towel and then suddenly without warning he took it in his hands and started feeling it. 'Did you not get enough last night?' I said to which he replied, 'No, never!' He then seemed to bend down and when he stood up I realised he had removed his shorts and was naked behind me.

His hands felt me up from behind, first my legs then my bum then he slid up inside the towel to feel my back before sliding them round to cup my breasts as he let out a grunt. I continued with my make up stopping occasionally as he squeezed my boobs hard in a somewhat frustrated manner. His dick was pressing hard against my backside, rubbing all over my cheeks and then down between my legs making me moist. He started rocking back and forth, his hard cock sliding back and forth along my clit. I dropped the make up and steadied myself ready his first thrust inside but I was too late and my head nearly hit the mirror. The second came quickly after the first pushing my face into the cold glass. I was ready for his third using my hand against the mirror to brace myself. By then the towel had completely left me and had fallen to the floor. I was naked and getting it hard from behind. Using my hands against the mirror I pushed back into him and twisted my thighs to get him deeper inside and to pleasure me more.

He fucked me hard, then harder and we battered against one another until a thought struck me, I hadn't taken the pill that morning nor the one before and I immediately used all my strength to push him off me exclaiming, 'You're not coming inside me!' 'Ah come on,' he said, 'you can't leave my like this'. 'You can come on my boobs,' I said as I knelt down in front of him.

He was clearly annoyed and frustrated but I took his penis in my hand and began licking it and tasting myself off him. I sucked down hard on his shaft and then gently licked it and kissed it. He didn't like the softly approach and grabbed my chin in one hand taking his dick in the other and started rubbing it in my face then hard into my mouth. I nearly choked at first he rammed it in so forcefully. Then as I looked up at him with my mouth open he began hitting my tongue with it whacking me as I knelt before him taking it. I didn't like it and I was afraid he would come in my face or my mouth so I raised myself up onto my knees and placed my breasts around his erection. Using my breasts I rubbed him up and down between them squeezing them tightly until he came. He came all over my chest, let out a groan and then walked out. I was left in the bathroom on my knees with his come all over my chest. What a morning!

Not much sunbathing was done that day in fact I spent most of my time inside. I felt uncomfortable at the pool because I couldn't look at him. The others were oblivious to it but I kept thinking about his dick in my face and it made me feel a little ashamed.

The following morning I went out early hoping he wouldn't be there. I knew he probably would be but as it was our last full day at the villa I wanted to spend most of it under the sun. It was a hot morning, hotter than normal and I felt the heat burning my bare feet as I stepped outside from the shade and onto the hot tiles by the pool.

The sky was light blue and bare. Void of all cloud as if the sun had dried up all the moisture in the air making it feel dry against the skin almost as if walking through a furnace and I had to remind myself it was only the morning sun.

The beautiful day was disrupted by his presence, already out there as usual, watching me approach. He sat smiling on his lounger greased with tanning lotion and his now very dark skin shimmered as the sun rays bounced off him as if he were covered in shiny foil.

'Great day' his small talk began. 'Hot' I said not wanting to appear keen to strike up a conversation. 'You got your own oil today then?' he remarked with a wry smile. 'Yes' I nodded as I dropped both my towel and book onto the lounger.

My short answers gave him more information that they stated. They told him I was not interested in chatting. In fact I hoped they told him that my interest in him was over.

As we lay there I felt it difficult to read my book bending the pages away from the glaring sun so as not to be blinded by its refection. My greasy fingers smudging the ink as drops of sweat fell periodically from my brow, blotting the copy further. It was already becoming too hot. Too hot to concentrate and I knew my body needed cooling down so I dropped the book and rose from my lounger sliding my hands behind me to adjust my bikini bottoms which had stuck to my bum.

I'm sure he studied my backside as I corrected my clothing and I felt his eyes burn into me as I walked towards the pool. I turned facing him before dipping a toe in. 'Can't be too cold' he shouted but I didn't answer as my leg was sliding in and the cool water was gripping my leg as if to draw me further into it.

As I walked down the steps the cool water slid up my legs as if a million hands were massaging them, gripping them tight and enticing me into the water. It was lovely, just what was required and before long I let my whole body fall into the water which know embraced my entire soul, cooling me, soothing me and taking away all the troubles in my mind. The thoughts of him and what he had done drifted away as the tranquil noise of gentle water waves lapped around me slapping the sides of the pool as I swam across it.

I had never been a great swimmer so the breast stroke suited me keeping my head just above the water and using my arms and legs to propel me slowly forward without much effort but just enough to glide across the pool. I reached the end closest to him and turned, without looking at him, making my way back to the other side. When I reached the side I pulled out my arms resting them crossed in front of me so I could lay my chin onto my hands. My arms held out of the water allowed me to hold my body there gently floating effortless and peaceful. Then I heard a splash and drops of water showered over my head. He was in the pool.

I could hear his splashing getting louder until I knew he was coming up behind me. I held myself there with my arms my feet just unable to touch the bottom. I didn't want to turn as I knew I would be facing him and eventually the warmth of his body was felt against my back just before his hands were felt on my belly before sliding around my now cooled body before groping me.

My gaze was fixed on the patio doors in front of me, the entrance to the villa and the exit for anyone coming out to the pool. His hands felt my breasts over my bikini squeezing them with vigour. The thought of being caught raced through my mind and I have to admit aroused me.

His hands slipped down right inside my bikini bottoms and I let out a moan as he slid his fingers up and down my clitoris. I was staring at the patio doors and thinking, what if someone comes out?

His fingers went inside me and that made me very horny. I was cool on the outside but burning with desire inside. I let my arms fall as I spun around to him, 'We can't do this here' I said looking into his eyes but his head turned and he leaned in to kiss me. He kissed my lips, then licked them, then slid his tongue inside all the while shuffling about down below, getting his penis out and moving my bikini to the side. He slid inside with his usual forcefulness pressing my back into the side on the pool and then whatever he did, however he did it. I fucking loved it! I loved him inside me like that with my legs wrapped around his waist as he dug upwards and deeper inside penetrating me deep and deeper. It was intense and fantastic. His dick was touching me inside in what can only be described as a very sensual spot, perhaps my G-spot? My eyes closed in ecstasy, my arms outstretched by my side and my hands formed fists attempting to hold onto the sides of the pool. His hands were under my bum holding me up and bouncing me up and down as his dick kept hitting that spot!

I believed I was in Nirvana and about to orgasm. I wanted to let go and come so badly but then I thought, what if he did? I didn't want his sperm inside me and as I had forgotten the pill a couple times I wasn't sure if I would be safe?

Once again I had to use all my strength to push him off. I pulled away and swam off. 'I told you, you can't come inside me'.

'Come back' he said but I replied, 'No, what if someone comes?'

It was lucky I did stop because sure enough as I was getting out of the pool my husband's sister and her boyfriend came walking out from those patio doors. 'You too having fun?' she said knocking me for six and leaving me embarrassed and therefore unable to reply so I just said, 'Hot today.'

But then at that moment I realised my legs were not working and I nearly fell back into the pool. I was weak at the knees, my legs were shaking and I had to use my hands to pull myself up and out of the pool instead of using the steps. My face seemed overly warm too, perhaps burnt by the sun or perhaps just embarrassed at nearly getting caught.

Before long everyone was out by the pool and I was getting burning sensations on different parts of my body. I was wary of how long I could keep re-applying oil before I would burn so I told my husband I was gonna get some washing done and start packing explaining my fears to him.

I first went to the bedroom and gathered up some dirty clothes before heading to the laundry room. I was bent over putting my things into the washing machine when I heard the door shut behind me. I didn't have to turn to know who it was. It had to be him, my stalker as I know referred to him in my head. Sure enough as I turned there he was all happy with himself standing in his swimming shorts and holding a condom. I knew what he wanted, why he had followed me, why he was holding a condom and as we weren't exactly fond of chatting so I said nothing.

I wanted him to penetrate me like he had done in the pool so I could feel him hitting that spot again so I slipped my bikini bottoms off and sat on the washing machine facing him. He walked over and manoeuvred himself in between my legs then dropped his shorts so he stood naked in front of me. He handed me the condom and I opened the wrapper.

He was already semi-hard at the thought of what would happen so I cupped his balls and gently massaged them watching him rise further before using my hand to stroke him harder. I placed the condom carefully on and turned my head to kiss him. As we kissed my hands felt all around his balls and his hands felt the inside of my legs and played with me, making me moist and getting me ready.

He started playing with the lips of my clitoris making me crave him and crave that feeling from before. He used his fingers to part my lips before sliding inside with ease as my body was still relaxed from our time in the pool. At first I enjoyed him thrusting into me as I arched my back and he kissed my neck as I presented it to him.

He untied my bikini top and took it off as he fucked me. Kissing, sucking and playing with my breasts as he went in and out but he never reached that spot. Then I couldn't wait any longer so I lunged myself forward off the washing machine and into his arms. My arms around his shoulders were holding me up whilst his hands soon found their place on my bum as he held me in position. He held me there and continued again and again until his thrusts finally hit the spot!

It was slightly different with the condom on but it was still ecstasy for me. He banged me like that for ages and I moaned louder and louder until I felt it, a thousand horses running over me, pounding my bones under hoof, pounding my body from my legs to my heart, pounding my heart before lifting and flying away leaving those waves from before lapping inside my veins like the water lightly crashing against the sides of the pool. The very blood in my veins felt like it was crashing gently inside my body. Then a lightness as if I myself was weightless but it was actually him setting me down onto the washing machine. His thrusting had subsided while I orgasmed allowing me to enjoy the moment before arousing him all over again. His stare became more determined. His will to come inside me grew even stronger, his character more forceful and just like the time before, after the shower, he had that dirty look on his face like he was evil, possessed even.

His strong hand pushed me backwards onto my elbows. He then lifted my legs up and pulled them up over his shoulders. I was nearly lying down on the washing machine and as his thrusts became more forceful with his hands still holding my thighs, he bucked his body into mine. His head lifted and I knew that was it. I felt it inside even though he was wearing a condom but I was so sensitive down below I felt his penis throb inside me as he came into the condom. I knew he was coming and pumping his sperm out just before he stopped.

He pulled out. 'That was great' he said. 'Yeah' I said suddenly happier than ever before at the though of him and me. 'I feel dizzy he said' and he stumbled back away from me and took off his condom. 'It's the heat I said' as I got up from the washing machine. We both stood there naked. Full carnal knowledge of each other we had yet we didn't know much else but at last a mutual respect was between us. He saw me as more than just a nice face, great tits and an ass he wanted to pound. I was a good shag, a great shag even and to him that was much more than just a pretty face. What did I see? I saw someone frustrated with his life but passionate. Someone needing a break away from his partner or perhaps someone who needed introduced to swinging? I started chatting to him about it as we both dressed but he said his Mrs would never go for it. He then kissed me, a lingering kiss on the lips and we left the room together before going our separate ways.

That was our last day at the villa and that night we partied in one of the local clubs after dinner.

He had finally stopped staring at me and watching me but I wasn't sure this pleased me. I think I wanted his attention and when it was gone I felt sad, lonely even. It sounds strange but I wanted to be wanted.

Later that night I remember sitting in the club looking around me. I saw my husband with this guy's wife on his knee. Innocent enough but I could tell she liked him and I wondered if she might be into swinging after all. My husband smiled over at me and I nodded back as if to say 'You and her?' but he gently shook his head without her noticing the exchange. She was busy rabbiting on about something and sipping her cocktail through a fancy twirly straw. To my immediate right was my husband's sister's boyfriend and his head looked as if it was about to fall off. He was nodding off and I thought to myself, what an appropriate term. His head nodded forward and then jolted back then nodded further forward. I think he was actually sleeping but then where was his girlfriend and where was my stalker? He certainly wasn't stalking me anymore!

I glanced over to the bar and saw him with his arm around my husband's very drunk sister. I watched him now as he had once watched me, my eyes now burning into his back as I sat there alone and again feeling lonely.

His hand slid down her back and onto her bum cheeks holding them gently as they chatted and laughed. I very nearly got up in a jealous rage until he lifted his hand again resting in the small of her back. Did she feel that? I wondered. Why am I getting jealous? I thought. Should I wake this guy beside me? Tell him what I saw? But there was no point in starting a row.

I just couldn't sit there on my own, however, watching him flirt with her. Not after what I saw next. He did it again. His hand dropped but this time he groped her ass. She felt that! I thought as I rose and began walking towards them with my eyes fixed on his hand but before I arrived she turned and began towards me with a drink in each hand.

'He's a laugh' she tipped a nod back in his discretion as she remarked to me in passing.

I kept on until I reached the bar green with envy.

'You buying the drinks?' I said, 'Want one?' he said, 'I'll have a deep throat' I smiled back at him in a flirtatious way but he signalled the barman and ordered without acknowledging my smile.

I downed it in one, 'Another' he said, 'Yes' was my reply as I slid my body closer to his. I wanted him to want me so badly. He seemed indifferent as he paid the barman and again I downed my drink in one. 'Take it easy' he said giving me licence to flirt again, 'You take me easy' I said as I slurred my words, it didn't come out right what was I saying. Fuck it, I thought I need to show him what I mean so I put my hand down and into his jeans. 'Steady on, are you drunk' was his reply and I felt annoyed, ashamed even. Why didn't he want me? then I felt the third shot kick in as I pulled out my hand and stumbled backwards. I don't remember anything more about that night!

I have, however, been reminded by my husband on many an occasion since that I sang loudly and out of tune all the way back to the villa, as he propped me up but I still remember nothing.

Our last day began with a flurry of activity. Once again I was last up with everyone else busy packing last minute items and tidying. My head was pounding as if a marching band was testing its instruments inside it, badly out of rhythm and to no recognisable tune.

Every cupboard door closing sounded like an explosion and the squeal from the wheels of the suitcases sounded like thousands of mice being horribly murdered.

My head was throbbing as if my temples were moving in and out as I walked. My mouth was so dry it felt void of all moisture, saliva, taste even and my tongue felt swollen and numb.

I shuffled into the kitchen, downed a pint of water along with headache tablets and turned on the kettle, 'Anyone want a cuppa?'

'No time love' was the reply 'We gotta be outa here in twenty minutes, you need to get ready'. 'Where are we gonna go?' I said sheepishly to which I heard a cry in unison, 'The beach!'

Our flight was not until much later that day and we are going to spend the day at the beach. Ah! I thought, throw on a bikini, jump in car, hit the beach and lie down. Lie down as soon as I could. Lie down, I thought again and then I would be fine.

My husband, bless him, had already packed our bags and had everything sorted. He even left me out a beach bag with towel, skirt, sun oil and bikini. I managed to get into my bikini just and hopped into the car.

The chatter inside the vehicle felt too loud but the beach was close so before long I was on a sun longer looking out to the beautiful ocean and lying down. Yes lying down at last. My headache had faded to a dull thud but was easing as the rays of sun warmed my body.

'Volleyball!' was the cry that disturbed me after an hour or so, 'No-way' said I shaking my head. The others ran to the sea and played in the sea for what seemed like forever stopping only for snacks at lunchtime. I was handed a hotdog at lunchtime which I ate without even lifting my head.

As the day wore on I began to realise who was playing volleyball. There were four of them so who was missing?

I sat up and looked around and there he was behind me. I should've known he would be also be sunbathing, catching the last of the holiday sun.

I sat up for a while glad to find that my headache was gone and I started to think about home. My thoughts turned to the flight and getting ready so I gathered my things together and headed off to the shower block.

It wasn't the nicest or cleanest of places and it seemed to be communal. There were toilets but no urinals and three separate shower cubicals. One was larger than the rest and in the corner. I picked that one so there would be room to throw down my clean clothes without them getting wet.

I went into the cubical and tuned on the shower. I was immediately hit with a blast of cold water that made my nipples stand to attention as they poked through my bikini top. I turned the dial until the water warmed and then I rubbed the soap together in my hands. I worked a lather up into my hands before rubbing it up my arms. I began rubbing out the sand and oil as I worked my way up to my shoulders until I heard a noise, the cubical door!

The locks were crap and easy to open from the outside but as it had to be opened I knew this had to be someone who wanted to come inside, someone wanting to come inside while I was inside, who knew I was there, someone like my stalker!

I was a little anxious, afraid maybe in case it was someone else but I stood firm and began again to create a lather with the soap in my hands. I felt his presence right behind me just like before in the shower room that morning he entered me for the first time and like before in the pool. This was his usual approach and I knew it was him, it had to be.

Two hands appeared in front of me and took mine in his. We both worked the soap into a frothy lather before his hands began rubbing my tummy as if he was washing me then they disappeared around my back up my back and onto my shoulders gently massaging them like the time he put sun tan lotion on them. It had to be him, didn't it?

My bikini top was then untied with his fingers and it dropped exposing my breasts. My nipples were still erect from the cold water or maybe it was because I was slowly becoming more and more aroused? Was it because I wasn't sure who this was or was it because I didn't know what would happen next? I wasn't sure but I was very horny and before I could answer myself his hands came back into view under my chest and back into my hands gathering more lather before cupping my breasts. He must have felt my hard nipples as he began sliding his hands all over my breasts. I moved my arms behind me and found he was naked. I used my soapy hands to pleasure him, feeling him and sliding up and down his rock hard penis. His hands were sliding all over my front then Wow! inside my bikini bottoms just like before. This must be him, we have been here before I thought but I still wasn't 100% sure. I couldn't tell by his penis, should I turn to him. I thought but as I asked myself he slipped away.

Where was he? What was he doing? I questioned. I then realised that he must have bent down because his soapy hands began sliding up my legs. It was just like the time I slipped into the pool, just like the water sliding up my legs but this time creating a warm sensation rather than the coolness of the pool. He pulled my bottoms off gently before massaging my bum, paying attention to every inch of my skin and occasionally sliding his hand between my legs teasing me as he slid past.

This was divine, a great hangover cure, but what was my role? Would he fuck me from behind like the first time or would he fuck me like in the pool the way I liked? Was it even him? Who else? Was it my husband?

I was still unsure but I let the pleasure engulf me so that I didn't care as his fingers slipped inside and out quickly and he teased me more and more. Then I turned, I couldn't help it, and as I did I looked down to him kneeling in front of me and saw only the top of his head. It's not him, I thought at first but then he looked up and caught my eye, it was him, my stalker. I knew it was him all along, didn't I?

He looked at me as his mouth drew closer to my vagina before his tongue came out and he began licking my clitoris. My hands fell by my side and dropped the soap. My hands then made fists squeezing out the soapy suds as his tongue lashed against my lips and tickled me. He picked up the soap as he stood up allowing his hands to feel the backs of my legs and then my bum as he groped his way all over me. I enjoyed his touch and felt his hands as they worked their way up my back and then around to my front which was also slipping and sliding against his then he leant in and snogged me. We snogged like that for ages as we allowed both of our hands to wander all over each other with ease.

He then lifted my left leg in his right hand and pulled me towards him. His erect penis was inches away from being inside me. I slid my hand down and grabbed it rubbing it furiously with my soapy fingers and watched his face as he too was filled with ecstasy. I pulled it into me so that the tip was on my hot wet soapy lips. His knob felt warm against the lips of my clitoris and he understood the invitation as he pushed it inside. The heat of his shaft pierced me as I'm sure the warmth inside me radiated through him. He pushed me forcefully back against the cold tiles as he fucked upwards into me. I wrapped my arms around his neck and lifted myself up, lifting my supporting leg off the ground which he caught. We were now in that position, the one from the pool, the one from the laundry room, the one I enjoyed and the one that meant his knob would hit that spot again and it surely did.

I was afraid I would slip out of his grasp but the wall supported me as he fucked me, kissing, slipping and fucking. That spot was hit over and over and this time I moaned in fact I yelled quite loudly in fact 'That's it', 'Right there' 'Oh yes' 'Fuck me' 'Fuck me' 'Fuck me harder' my words turned him on sending him wild and bringing out that dirty demonic side as he banged me up against the wall.

'You like that?' 'Like that huh?' 'Yes! Yes!' I exclaimed. 'Take that you Fuck! You Fucking Slag' 'Take that you Bitch' 'You Dirty Bitch'. His words sent a chill down my spine and I said nothing more. He continued 'Fucking Cunt! I'm gonna come inside you this time you Slut', 'Dirty Bitch I wanna come in you' 'In your face' my moans turned to cries, 'AHH' 'AHH' nearly sore as he furiously fucked me, my back hurting as it hit hard against the wall and the pipes at times. 'You're a Fucking Whore' he exclaimed as he finally came inside me.

I was overwhelmed by the sensation caused by his dick and a culmination of the sensational and the pain I was enduring made me grit my teeth as he came and I dug my nails into his back. Perhaps it was to cause him some pain too or perhaps just to help ease some of mine. He came and seemed to come again maybe bucking out the last remaining liquid into me but as he finished he dropped me almost onto the floor. He turned and walked away and I slid down onto my backside to watch him put on his shorts and leave.

As I sat there naked with the shower still on and raining onto the back of my head I thought about what he said and the words he had been using. I felt his sperm leak out of me and I wondered about what I had become. I thought about the holiday from the first day when we met. I thought about how I had let another man who I didn't even know rub oil all over me. Was that ok? Was there anything wrong in that?

Then I thought about the kiss, I should never have let him kiss me after he had used my hand to have a wank. Was I a tart? A whore? Or those other words he used? What had I become?

Then I felt queasy as I recalled the incident the following day. I felt my back shudder as I sat there retching trying to stop myself from being sick remembering his dick in my face and how disgusting it made me feel.

I was a dirty bitch, a slut? Wasn't I? This was meant to be fun and I had fun in the pool and enjoyed the way he made me feel when I had the orgasm in the laundry room but what was I after? An orgasm at any expense? At the expense of my dignity, my marriage even? The last of his liquid oozed out of me as I stood up. I scrubbed myself with the soap no longer washing away the sand and oil but the dirt I felt on me, his dirt, my dirt. I didn't know for sure I just wanted to wash away the holiday. To wash away my regrets at all those times I went behind my husband's back but maybe even before that, before the villa when it had all started? My husband's boss or maybe even before that? The elderly man even or perhaps the guy I had on my kitchen counter?

Every thought went through my head as I scrubbed my skin, every seedy moment, every encounter, every orgasm I chased and more besides.

I got on the plane behind my husband following his lead. He sat at the window and, as always, I sat next to him. The plane was filing up and I thought, who will sit beside me? Surely not him? He will be beside his wife? But the plane filled and there was no sign of either of them. Then the last passengers got on I willed someone to take the seat next to me, someone, anyone?

I should've known as my stalker sat next to me.

My husband stared out the window during take-off unable to hear him whispering in my ear, 'Lets do it on the plane, in the toilets? Join the mile-high club?' My husband couldn't see my head shaking in defiance or see my mouth as my lips exaggerated the word 'NO' on three separate occasions. My stalker continued to badger me as we flew.

My husband eventually fell asleep as most other people did. It was dark by then and the cabin was very quiet except for his continued whispering, 'C'mon, why not?' 'No' I said out loud so he could not be mistaken this time. But I felt him search for my hand and find it taking it over to his lap. He pushed my hand between his legs and started rubbing himself using my hand. His whispering continued in my ear, 'I wanna fuck you, dirty bitch.' I don't know if he came but he rubbed for ages while I looked away. I watched my husband as he slept and I realised as I watched him that I didn't want this anymore, this secret or not so secret life and all this mucking around. My swinging days were definitely over and my playing away over too.

As my mind wandered and I sat alone on that plane I began to examine what had got me to that point, why I had let myself become an object of desire for men, why I had let myself and my body be used in this way. Perhaps it was because my father died when I was so young?

I felt starved of male attention when I was young and I sought it in the most depraved of ways. I couldn't blame this on the loss of my dad, could I?

Perhaps it was down to the way my friends treated me when I was a teenager? I didn't know for sure and couldn't pin point the moment in my life that made me this way. All I knew was that I wanted it to stop. Looking for that Boxing Day moment was silly and I was looking in the wrong places. It wasn't sex that made that time special it was love. The love that blossomed between my husband and I. Had I forsaken that love or let myself forget it?

I wasn't prepared to take any more chances in fear I might loose what I had and right there right then I decided it was over.

That plane journey became a personal journey waiting to touch me down onto the ground and into a new life. One where we would be settled and no longer exploring. I was intent on confronting my husband about this and do you know what? I did.

That incident on the plane was my last as a swinger.

About the Author

Nicci Greene gives us an amazing account of her story and tells it in erotic detail. She is an accomplished author with three books all of which chart her extrordinary life. Her first published book, 'Confessions of a Swinger' takes us through her twenties and gives us an insight into the woman behind the story. She tells her tales in a romantic way with an easy to read literary style and in short chapters. Her ability to deliver punchy short individual erotic tales allows you to easily sink into her life story and to feel at one with the her as she takes us through the time when she married and then became a swinger. This is an author who writes from the heart and who can be read and enjoyed by both men and women alike. Nicci's writing differs from the traditional erotic novel and delivers a real story behind the passion, sex and intrigue.

If you enjoyed My Story and want to know what happened next pre-order your copy of my next book, 'Confessions of a Seductress' by sending your name address and contact details to niccigreene@live.co.uk

Nicci Greene

Printed in Great Britain
by Amazon.co.uk, Ltd.,
Marston Gate.